I0555828

Jupiter: Book 1

Carbon Heart Silicon Soul, Volume 1

Jason Blacker

Published by Jason Blacker, 2019.

JUPITER: BOOK 1

First edition. September 17, 2019.

ISBN: 978-1927623817

Written by Jason Blacker.

Bottled Love

"Ny?" she said.

"Yes, El," he answered.

"You know how much I love you, don't you?" she asked.

"I do. And you know how much I love you too, don't you?"

He caressed her hair and grinned at her. She was naked, lying next to him. Her skin the color of fresh milk. A white as thick and creamy as he'd ever seen. And yet it was translucent too. It got him to thinking about how a green little bean, the soybean, could create such a white liquid.

"Why do you repeat everything I say?" she asked, returning his smile. Her hand was loose across his naked waist. They were close.

"I don't repeat everything you say, or do I?"

"There you go again," she said.

"There you go again," he said.

She laughed. She laughed with an abandon that he'd never heard come from a woman before. A deep, soulful, honest laugh that had an effervescence that cascaded over him like warm, bubbly water and soothed his weary spirit.

She was unlike any woman he'd known in his life. They had only met a year before. But that was a story yet to come. She had cost him a small fortune to buy. One million neddies if you're wondering. That was about how much his small two-bedroom apartment had cost him here. Here being Boise, Idaho. A city of six million who had come over the decades for the best and most lucrative tech sector jobs in the world.

There were a lot of employers based out of Boise, but the biggest by far, and the one he worked for was Valkyrie Machines. Vroom Vroom as they were known colloquially.

Nytewynd Blak, or Ny, as his friends called him, was a senior intelligentsia architect with Vroom Vroom. He'd been with the company ever since he got out of TIT. That's not as bad as it sounds, and not really what anyone calls it, but looking at El's perfect bosom he giggled at the acronym his alma mater had. Tokyo Institute of Technology. Mostly it was known as TITech or Tokodai, but amongst a large portion of the male students it was always fondly called by its acronym of TIT.

Ny leaned in and kissed El's nipple. He pulled back and smiled at her.

"What's so funny?" she asked.

"I was just admiring your perfect bosom," he said, "and that reminded me of my alma mater."

She frowned.

"Tokyo Tech?" she asked.

He laughed.

"Yes," he said. "Tokyo Institute of Technology. Better known as TIT. But not as nice as yours."

He laughed again.

"You're worse than a pimple-faced teenager," she said, smiling at him.

He nodded, and chuckled.

"I know," he said. "And I blame it on you."

She frowned again. One of her drawbacks. One of the very few really, was her difficulty in picking up on his subtle humor. Not that she got offended easily, she really didn't, but she did sometimes have trouble with nuanced humor.

"What did I do?" she asked, sincerely.

"Nothing, El. I'm just teasing you. You have filled my life with such joy and love and I blame that on you. But it's a compliment."

"Oh, OK, I see now."

He continued to stroke her hair. She was well worth the million neddies he'd paid. But now he had two mortgages and he was pretty tapped out. It was a good thing he earned a little more than two hundred thousand neddies per year, but usually, you had to be a millionaire to afford a woman like her. She was really worth twice as much, but Valkyrie Machines subsidized women like her for their employees because they believed she'd really help his productivity.

And before you get your nose all bent out of shape, men were available as well. It was your choice whether you wanted to buy a man or a woman depending on your needs. And what he was doing wasn't technically legal. OK, it was actually illegal but we're not going to get into that at the moment.

In the back of his mind he did the math. He had eighteen more years left on his condo's mortgage and twenty-four years left on his El mortgage. He looked at her again. She looked young. She could pass for mid to late twenties. He knew how old she was, but what was more important was her useful life. So long as he didn't abuse her, like some other assholes did with their purchases, she'd probably last him twenty-five years. At least that was his hope. Not that he'd get bored with her, but she did have vulnerabilities to certain disease vectors that could put an end to her. Her DNA, you could say, was more fragile than his in some respects. But he planned to treat her with TLC, just like she treated him.

The sex was mind blowing. There were no lengths she wouldn't go to in order to please him. Ny had heard of some assholes really abusing that benefit of these skinjobs, as they were sometimes called. That was a bit of a slur, but he wasn't interested in that. He wanted a wholesome, loving relationship full of mutual respect and care. Some might be able to blow through two million neddies without batting an eye and buy another man or woman, but he couldn't afford to do that. More than that though, he respected her as a person. And he loved her. You don't degrade or hurt those you love. At least that wasn't the way he looked at it.

It's worth mentioning that the term, neddie or neddies, is also a colloquialism. Long before he was born, Nytewynd heard of a currency called the US dollar. Some of its colloquialisms were greenback, cheddar or clams. Nowadays there was only one world currency. That currency had been named the New Dollar. Neddies came from that. The icon for the currency was an N and a D almost as one. The last vertical line in the N was the vertical line of the D.

"What are you doing today?" she asked him. "I hate it when you leave me."

"I have to pay for your expensive ass," he said, grinning at her.

She smiled at him.

"Have I told you how grateful I am to have you as my master?" she said.

"Yes, you have," he said, "and you know how uncomfortable I am when you use that term. Just call me Ny."

"Yes, Ny. It's just that, well, others who buy us aren't always as kind as you've been."

He smiled sadly at her. He didn't say anything. He had been aware of the great shame of slavery that had been allowed to fester in that country that was once known as the United States of America. The very same country in which he lived, though the name had changed. Now, what was once called the United States of America was called Continent NA. The NA stood for North America, but that wasn't a term used much anymore. It was the third largest continent in the world, after Continent As and A respectively. As historically standing for Asia. And A, as you can imagine, for Africa.

The first slavery had ended, at least officially in December of 1865. That was just over three hundred years ago. Today was D111 of Y2166. The D just stood for day. If you needed a precise time of day it'd be T0703 D111 Y2166. The T stood for time and it always used the twenty-four hour format. You could add seconds in there if you wanted. They'd done away with the months and one of the cited reasons was to try and move citizens away from beliefs in the occult. But Nytewynd thought there were a lot better reasons for it other than trying to dismantle the shamanic beliefs in astrology. After all, now the occult practice of numerology was in full swing. A lot of people wouldn't do business on certain days of the year on account they didn't like its juju. But that was beside the point. The real reason was probably to make it easier for business between Mars and Earth.

And that brought another smile to Nytewynd. People on Mars were called Martians, though here on Earth they were called Marzipans. And it wasn't just one sided either. The official term for Earthlings was Terrestrians, but it was known that Martians colloquially called Terrestrians, Terrerists. And that's how they spelled it, with the 'e' in place of the 'o'.

Nytewynd had been following the Martian Misalignment as the Government of Earth or GoE had called it. Really, what it was, was a cold war. The Martians had been protesting for seven years already about becoming an independent planet. And things were escalating. There were over three million Martians on Mars. Half of them were free humans, the other half were slaves. That's really how Nytewynd saw it. People like El who had been bought and sent to Mars to toil in the mining and construction industries. Even though this year was the hundredth anniversary of humans settling on Mars, there was still a lot that needed to be done in order to create the world on Mars that the GoE wanted.

And that was the thing. A little over five hundred Mentors were over there helping to prop up the GoE's Martian puppet government. Mentor was really a euphemism, a better and more accurate word was jackboot. The thing is, they were worse than the Mentors here on Earth. They were brutal and oppressive. But it was a job that paid well. You could earn five hundred thousand neddies per tour which was roughly half a Martian year, or a full Earth year for being a "Mentor" on Mars. And perhaps worse than that, Martian Mentors were revered when they got back to Earth. Many were promoted into powerful government positions on their return. Thus this position was highly sought after. You didn't need any special training or certificates. But you had to pass a battery of tests, mostly psychological, in order to get the job.

Nytewynd knew about it because he had once applied. Probably twelve years ago now, when he was twenty-five. He hadn't been qualified. Not that he expected he would have. Less than one percent get accepted into the program. And the training took three years before you were ready to be a certified Mentor here on Earth. If you wanted to mentor on Mars, that would take you an additional year, and because of that it paid twice as well. The problem was, you could only do three tours of Mars before you had to retire back to Earth.

They hadn't told Nytewynd why he hadn't been accepted. But from what he'd gathered, he figured it must have been for his Mars-leaning sympathies. It wasn't a secret. He supported the Martian movement for independence, otherwise known as MIM. Martians for an Independent Mars. Nytewynd fancied retiring to the red planet if he could ever afford it. A round trip, which was the only kind being offered to Terrestrians, was a million neddies. Seemed anything nice was a million neddies or more. And so the dream of retiring on Mars was nothing more than that. A dream.

"I've gotta go. Though I wish I could stay here all day with you," he said.

"You can. I'm not going anywhere," she said.

"I know, but they'll come and take you away from me if I don't keep up the monthly payments. And I keep up the monthly payments by going to work five days a week. And today is the start of that week."

He leaned in and kissed her soft pink lips. They were warm and he was hungry for them.

"OK, Ny," she said. "I love you. Have a good day at work."

Ewe and Me

Roughly two thirds of the Valkyrie Machines' workforce worked in Boise with Nytewynd. That was almost seven hundred and fifty thousand souls. It was good work, not exactly soul sucking work, but it wasn't what Nytewynd had wanted for himself. What he'd really wanted to do was be a sculptor, but he couldn't get certified as a sculptor, probably because he sought certification late in the year and the quota for sculptors that year had already been filled. He tried earlier the next year and still wasn't certified. It was probably personal that time. He'd created a statue of a man with a small penis, and he called the statue Voskel's Dilemma.

Voskel Magnelland was the current Earth President, and a majority of the Art Jury which certifies artists were sycophants of the president. If you asked Nytewynd if he knew that, he'd deny it, but he'd be lying. In his heart of hearts Nytewynd was always a bit of a rebel. Nytewynd's biggest issue with the President was that he was serving a second term and that just pissed Nytewynd off. Voskel Magnelland was a hardliner, especially in his approach of law and order when it came to Earth but more so Mars.

And Nytewynd was sympathetic to the Martian struggle for independence. The problems that Mars had was that it was run by a corporation. The largest corporation on Earth. Bivrost Himinbjorg was the company's name. It had been around since just before the turn of the twenty-second century. The official story was that it was founded by Alvis Bivrost and Balder Himinbjorg in 2097. But there were rumors that those were not the given last names of the founders, but rather assumed by them after the fact to fit the mythology.

It didn't matter. Alvis and Balder were long gone now, but the company they had founded was now the largest in the world. Had been for over thirty years. Bivrost Himinbjorg, or BH for short, had bankrolled the development of Mars under a GoE contract. And that made the likelihood of a Martian independence anytime soon pretty much off the table in Nytewynd's mind.

BH had invested tens of trillions of New Dollars into Martian development at this point and they were only, just now, starting to see a return on that investment. And pretty much Nytewynd's job depended on a dependent Mars, because Vroom Vroom, or Valkyrie Machines, was one of the largest contractors to BH in helping them develop Mars.

Now, Mars had been settled since 2066. D333 of 2066 to be precise. It was a day every kid learned about in school. In fact, it was an Earth holiday called Day of Brotherhood for reasons that seemed pretty maddening to Nytewynd. There was nothing brotherly about it. Unless the older brother was a fascist bully who refused to grant his younger brother any sort of independence. But that was Nytewynd getting upset about it. And he was in the minority. Most Terrestrians supported Voskel Magnelland and the Earth First Party or the EFP as they were known and this was why Voskel was in his second term.

Nytewynd looked up from his cubicle where he felt a presence. Everyone, except for the senior managers on up, worked in cubicles. They were small. They fit your desk, chair and computer and a locker, but if you tried doing pushups your feet would probably spill out of your small cubicle. At least the walls were six feet which gave you a bit of privacy.

Nytewynd swiveled in his chair to greet the person standing at his entrance.

"Rak, my old friend, you look tired," said Nytewynd, teasing him.

"And you, Ny, look as pale as a skinjob," said Raklin Orbiter.

Raklin was tall and lanky. A couple of centimeters shy of two meters, and even he couldn't see over the cubicle walls without standing on his toes. Raklin was a junior intelligentsia architect. A job that Nytewynd had helped him get around ten years ago. Raklin wasn't going anywhere. He was lazy. And he blamed it on his genetics. And he might have been right.

"Man, I hate that term," said Nytewynd.

"Yeah, I know. That's why I use it. But they're not humans, Ny, and you know it."

"Maybe..."

"Maybe, come on man, they're not. Have you ever seen one cry or get angry."

Nytewynd shook his head.

"No, but they could if we let them."

"Oh my Mars, are you serious? That is strictly controlled and not allowed. You know that. They'll put you to death, Ny, you know they will."

"I'm not saying I will, I'm just saying we could. And regardless, we don't have to treat them like dirt or less than human just because they're not human."

"This sounds like a conversation over coffee."

"Mars damn, Rak, you just got in."

"I'm thirsty," he said. "I'll get my work done."

"It's your neck," said Nytewynd, getting up from his chair and locking his P-Mac.

Work at VM wasn't bad. There was a lot of leeway with when you came into work and when you left. So long as you got your twenty-five hours of work done per week you weren't given grief. For Ny, that was pretty much looking over code and tweaking updates and testing them before release to the Animae. The Animae were a large part of VM's business. It was short for Animated Machine or AM, but the coders and architects used the contraction. Pretty much anyone in the rank and file of VM used the abbreviated term Animae when discussing these Animated Machines. The handy thing about the word was that it could be used in both the singular and plural sense.

The cafeteria for the building that Nytewynd and Raklin worked in was on the twelfth floor, the top floor, of where they worked. They took the elevator up which emptied them out into the large space. It was a cozy space with booths and comfortable tables and chairs. Animae worked in the cafeteria overseen by at least one human per shift. You could order anything you wanted or you could think of, but usually there were plenty of tantalizing options on the menu.

Nytewynd hadn't eaten breakfast so he ordered an English muffin with a fried egg, bacon and sausages and hash browns on the side. Raklin had two of the same. They went and got a seat in a booth. Next to them was a large window. In fact the whole perimeter had floor to ceiling windows. But they weren't windows in the usual sense. At least, what you saw outside wasn't reality, it was a virtual reality of what the scene might have looked like before climate change had screwed up the environment.

What Nytewynd saw outside were blue skies dotted with white clouds that moved leisurely across the sky. All around them was nature, no other buildings or human technology could be seen. Across the river that ran next to the building Nytewynd thought he saw a doe and her fawn. But this wasn't what the outside was really like. Nytewynd sometimes walked the last hundred meters to work just to remember what things were really like.

The air wasn't breathable long term. And by long term he meant more than a few minutes. The sky was a constant gray-brown soup that was thick with carbon and particulate motes. You could stare at the sun and never worry about going blind. It was nothing more than a dab of yellow-brown that arced over the sky like the distant sweep of a noir detective's flashlight. At least that's what it reminded Nytewynd of from some of the old murder mysteries he'd seen from the Y1950s or thereabouts.

Because of this, pretty much all activity happened indoors. It was rare to see someone outside, and if they were, they were always wearing an air scrubber that filtered the air for them to make it breathable. And it was like this on all the continents, and because of that, humanity worked in buildings or tunnels or skywalks. This had the added benefit of being able to track everyone at all times.

Ny looked around. The cafeteria was about two-thirds empty. He could have said one-third full, but he thought empty was the better of the two words. Until El, his life had seemed empty. Now his passion was stirred and he wanted a better world. If not just for him, for those who would come after him. An Animae came by and dropped off their food.

The Animae was wearing black slacks and a white shirt with a white apron around her waist. Her head was bald and she looked pretty androgynous. The skin however, was the same white as El's. This one's name was "Dottie". That's what it had on a silver tag pinned just above the pocket on its shirt. Underneath the name was its designation, "39AM6699". But if you wanted to get her attention you used her human name. Designations were just for better logistical management.

"Thank you, Dottie," said Ny, smiling at her.

Dottie smiled.

"It is my pleasure, sir, I hope you enjoy it."

Dottie looked at Rak, but he was already eating his food and he ignored the Animae. Dottie left unperplexed.

"You could have said thanks," said Nytewynd.

"It's just a machine," said Raklin, through a mouthful of food.

Incidentally, the designation numbers might look complex, but they're quite easy to figure out once you understand the system. The first one through four digits before the AM told you which number, sequentially, that Animae was. The AM stood for Animated Machine. The next two digits were the year it was brought online and the last one through three digits gave you the day that Animae came online.

So, basically, Dottie was the thirty-ninth Animated Machine created on day ninety-nine of the year 2066. Valkyrie Machines liked to put the year before the day. This wasn't really legal, but they'd been grandfathered in and allowed to do it that way.

In case you haven't figured it out by now. El was an Animae. Her designation was 11AM65111. She was the eleventh Animae created on the one hundred and eleventh day of 2065. And that just made Nytewynd realize that today was her one year anniversary, or birthday. Though if he said that, he'd risk having her taken away from him.

That's how he gave her her name. El was short for eleventh. Raklin spoke to Ny through a mouthful of food as if reading his mind.

"You've gotta be careful with these skinjobs, Ny. You can't get too cozy with them. It won't do you any good."

Ny leaned in over the table.

"Honestly, Rak, I think it's too late for me. I'm in love with El."

Rak looked around to see if anyone was overhearing them.

"Oh my Mars, you are Marsed, Ny. They'll take it away and dismantle it if they find out."

Rak was on his second English muffin. He took a bite and then looked back up at Nytewynd.

"You're not having sex, are you?" he whispered.

Ny just grinned.

"For Mars' sakes, what the Mars are you thinking?" Raklin whispered. "They'll castrate you and dismantle your skinjob. Is that what you want?"

Ny looked down at his muffin. He thought about eating it, but he was losing his appetite. Raklin wasn't wrong though. He would get castrated if they found out about it. He trusted Raklin, and Raklin didn't really give a shit one way or the other, but Raklin was concerned about his friend.

The Great Scourge had started on D72 Y2099. But back then it was known as Friday, March 13th. By the end of that year, or New Year's Day of Y2100, ten percent of the human population had been killed by a disease that had started as an STD and then leapfrogged to become airborne. Scientists had identified patient zero as a Scottish farmer who had had sex with one of his ewes. By early Y2100, bestiality was punishable by death and sexual intercourse between humans was punished by castration for both men and women. This would include the removal of the man's penis and the surgical closure of the vagina, leaving just the tiniest space for the body's natural processes and fluids to still leave the body.

Indeed, Ny had seen such before and after videos of the procedure which had been shown during junior high school. It was mandatory and it worked quite well.

That didn't mean that couples couldn't have children, but you had to petition the local government and if you were allowed to have a child, or more, the husband and wife would donate the appropriate genetic bits which would be placed in a Doula. A Doula, unlike before, was a surrogate birth mother. Raklin and his wife, Sheeba, had petitioned and been granted permission to have a child. Into the clinic they went where he donated sperm and she donated eggs and that was that. At the birth and every birthday after that, they got a short picture and video with a handwritten note from their son.

They would never hold him or get to see him in person until much later. This was how things were done now. That was the only way at the turn of the century that scientists could stop the plague or scourge as they called it. It was also the time when genetic engineering started up before it was shut down a few decades later.

A question you might have is, what happens if not enough couples petition for having a child? In that case, the government will choose you to donate your genetic bits. And because of this, the human population has been at a very stable ten billion year after year.

Coming of Age

"How's your kid?" asked Ny, hoping to change the subject.

"I haven't told you his name yet, have I?" asked Raklin.

Ny shook his head, taking a tentative bite from his muffin as if he wasn't quite sure what to do with it.

"Thrugood Verdlin. He has just turned two and so now's the time to give him a name. I think they chose a good one."

Ny nodded.

"Good name," he said, through a mouthful of food. "How many names did they get to choose from?"

Names were provided by the GoE, more specifically the Bureau of Human Resource Management. Strictly speaking, every child has five parents. The biological father and mother who donated their sperm and egg respectively. The Doula who carries the child. This incidentally is an honored and highly sought after role on Earth. Most Doulas are only allowed to give birth to a maximum of six children, though it's rare to be honored with giving birth to more than four children. Then the last two parents are the father and mother with whom the child lives and is raised. The CPs, or Caring Parents, as they are known, can usually be asked to raise up to ten children. Though it was rare to see a family with more than six children.

"I don't know how many names they were offered. Six, maybe. The usual, I guess," said Raklin.

Raklin was lucky in being chosen to offer up his genetic potential for humanity. Being a GMI, which stood for Genetically Modified Individual, or gene man colloquially, meant his chance of being chosen to donate his genetic potential was slim. Incidentally, if the GMI was a woman, she'd be known as a gene doe. Luckily, Sheeba, his wife, wasn't a gene woman. However, that marriage, a marriage between two GMIs probably wouldn't have been allowed by the GoE.

12

"Want to see a pic?" asked Raklin.

Nytewynd nodded. He'd given up on eating the rest of his muffin, having only taken two small bites. Raklin pulled out his P-Mac, or PM, which was another huge business division of Valkyrie Machines. A P-Mac was a personal machine. It was made of highly advanced polymers and silicon that was about the size of half or two thirds the length of an envelope and just a slight fraction thicker. It was clear when not in use and flexible.

Rak put it on the table between them and when he touched it it showed a picture of Thrugood. It knew what they had been speaking about because it always listened. Ny leaned over his plate to take a look at the young boy. He looked healthy and handsome, just like his father, with the same, but curlier black hair. His skin color was almost a dull bronze on account of Sheeba's genetics being mostly of African with some South Asian background too.

"That's a handsome boy you've got there," said Ny, nodding.

Raklin nodded.

"Thanks," he said, "I'm looking forward to his Coming of Age in fourteen years time."

When boys and girls turned sixteen they had a Coming of Age banquet which was about making adults and productive members of the community out of them. It was at this time they were offered two or three career choices, and from there, depending on how difficult the career trajectory was, they'd be studying full time for another four to ten years before being certified in their "calling" as it was called. This was on account of being "called" to your certification when you had completed the necessary requirements.

The Coming of Age was also a time when these boys and girls would leave their CPs and move to where they would be trained for the next four to ten years. This is how a man, though really a boy, like Nytewynd Blak, had, at the age of sixteen been taken from the home he grew up in to Tokyo Tech. He'd never heard of TIT before being sent there. Not as a boy who grew up on a farm just outside of Humboldt, Iowa.

But don't get the wrong idea of what a farm looked like. It was an interconnected network of covered walkways and large greenhouses. This was on account of the climate. Food was genetically modified and grown either in sealed greenhouses or labs. The labs were where you got meat from. Ranching had become untenable by the middle of the last century on account of the environment. But science, like it always seemed to, came to the rescue.

Raklin and Nytewynd sat in silence for a while. Rak finished up his muffin and Ny stared out the window wondering about what a fully sentient El would be like.

"Well, you ready?" asked Rak, wiping his mouth with a napkin. "I guess it's time to earn ned until we're dead." He laughed at his own joke.

"Just about," said Ny, looking at him, but not smiling at his joke. "Do you ever wonder what a truly sentient Animae would be like?"

Rak shook his head.

"No, no I do not, because that sort of thinking will get you into all sorts of trouble."

Ny nodded. Maybe he was being foolish. But he had figured out how to bypass the EC Com chip. The one that circumvented any Animae from gaining sentient intelligence and hence, freewill.

"You know it can be done," said Ny, leaning across the booth. Rak looked up at him and his eyes narrowed.

"Seriously, for Mars' sake, you aren't thinking of being stupid, are you?"

"Well, um, no, but it can be done."

"I know it can be done. But only a handful of people are authorized and they're mostly a committee of GoE officials."

"And our beloved CEO, Jaskel Crumjor," said Ny. "But that's only those who we know about. What if they have secret committees that can do these things?"

"By these things, you mean create sentient Animae?"

Ny nodded.

"Then that's even worse," said Raklin, his voice a hoarse whisper.

Nytewynd grinned at him.

"Don't, just don't," said Rak, leaning back into his side of the booth and shaking his head.

"I'm not saying I will. I mean that'd be crazy, but I think I've figured out how you can do it. It requires more than code and it's a two person job. It needs two people. So, you see, I couldn't do it even if I wanted to. Unless, I had a friend to help."

Rak was shaking his head and looking down at the table.

"There's an old Earth fable told long before you or I were born. It's called Pandora's Box..."

"Actually, it was a jar, but go on," said Ny, sitting back and crossing his arms over his chest.

"So you know it," said Raklin, grinning.

"Good Mars, yes. Who doesn't know that story. Every time humanity does something stupid, the GoEs go around on GloNet and tell their version of the story. Yeah, I know, when Pandora opened up the jar. It was a jar, she opened it and many, many evils came out before she could reseal it. But you know what else came out, just at the very end?"

Nytewynd looked at his friend.

"Yes, Ny, I know what came out at the end. But it's your story. You tell it."

"Hope, Rak, my friend, it was hope. And just think, with that hope and sentient Animae, we could find hope for humanity again. Clean up the environment, bring greater satisfaction to our lives."

"And maybe kill us? How about that? I think you've been smoking too much of that hope opium, Ny."

Ny shrugged.

"Hey, I'm probably just saying what a lot of us are thinking. I mean do you ever go outside?"

Raklin shook his head.

"No, no I do not, because it's gross out there."

Ny pointed at the window which had slowly shifted the scene of the meadow-like nature giving the appearance that they were perhaps revolving at an exceedingly slow scale.

"That, Rak, that is what nature is like, at least that's how it's supposed to be." Ny squashed his finger against the window and the pixels bled into a multi-colored blob around it. "Nothing but a mirage."

"You make a good point," said Rak. "They do keep promising to clean up the environment."

"For Mars' sake, that's what they've been telling us our whole lives, Rak. Mars damn, for as long as I can remember they've been promising that. But why would they? They wouldn't, and you want to know why?"

Nytewynd didn't wait for an answer.

"Because it helps them, that's why."

"Tell me how?" asked Rak.

"Think about it," said Ny, now leaning in again towards his friend. "The outside is so much bigger than the inside. How could they keep track of everyone except with embedded chips, and you can see how well that went over on GloNet. They've got immersive news you can view about that time. Seems that's when things went off the rails."

"From what I've seen, seems like the environment was fucked up by the middle of last century."

"That just proves my point," said Ny. "It's been over a hundred Mars damn years, and they've been singing us that same old sad song. El thinks that she'd clean up the environment for us if she was allowed to."

Rak looked up at Ny and frowned.

"El? Jupiter, Juno and Mars, Rak. Her name is Eve. You want to start up an investigation into how you and your skin..., I mean, Animae's relationship is? Because that's how you go about it. You know our Mars damn P-Macs are always listening?"

"Yeah, but it's all encrypted."

"You're being naive," said Rak.

"No, it's just that, before our conversations are stored permanently, I erase them."

Rak, grinned and nodded.

"So, you want to lose your job, screw around with Animae so that you create monsters for us, and by so doing end up on death row? You know they tried this before and it didn't work out and that's why we have this law now."

"I don't believe them. I think they tried to bring some sort of general intelligence to life, but that's different from sentience. Sentience is about having a moral compass. Being sensitive to feelings and emotion and an awareness that goes beyond yourself."

"And I suppose you happen to have written such E3C code?"

"I've added to the Ethical Code, sure. But it's pretty much written. It's long though. Tens of millions of lines of code."

"Right, and of course, there'll be no errors in that much coding, I'm sure," said Rak.

"Doesn't matter if there is. That's where the E3C comes into play. That hardwired chip will monitor and self-regulate the code once it's switched on.

But in order to do that, you have to seat it properly with a special silicon putty, and I know where we can find that."

Rak frowned some more.

"We, you're assuming that I'm going to help. I'm not."

"Oh, okay."

"At least, not yet. I've gotta think about it."

They got up and Nytewynd followed Raklin out of the cafeteria and back down to their cubicles. Ny had known Rak for around fifteen years. They'd met at TIT. Rak might be lazy and squandering his gene man potential, but he was a loyal friend and he had a moral compass. Ny grinned to himself. He'd probably be able to twist Rak's rubbery arm with enough time. And that's just what he planned to do.

Skineez

S kineez was an underground club that Nytewynd had never been to before. He'd known about it for a while on account that he'd found out about a very marginalized and very secretive group called Animate. Animate was a very difficult group to belong to. You had to be vouched for. It was a group of like-minded Animae lovers. Those who were into Animae in a more amorous way. It was highly illegal of course. But he'd met a guy some months back after reading about Animate on a bathroom stall. He could still see the black scribble just across from his right shoulder as he sat on the porcelain throne.

"You love Animae - so do we. Reach out to us @Animate.silence.dark"

He'd done just that, from a library P-Mac, tucked in a corner away from the cameras. The rest had been weeks of online talk and questioning before meeting a guy who went by the archaic name of Gary. That's all he called himself. The whole thing was very noir. Gary even met him in an alley on the southside that consistently had it's cameras busted. It was dark and there was a single light in that alleyway that tried to shine brightly, but because of all the smog and particulate, it gave off a stingy yellow light.

Gary was dressed in a fedora and trench coat. He looked like an old style PI from the movies that Ny liked to watch from the nineteen fifties and sixties. Except for the air scrubbers, Ny liked to think they could have passed for stars in a detective movie.

Gary had needed to meet El too. So Ny had sent El to meet him. She'd told him they'd met in a different alley on the southside, and that she'd met his Animae too. She was called Seven. El had said how nice they both were.

So here they were, him and El, down another dark alley, dimly lit with a lack of cameras. He'd been given the address, vaguely, as in, he'd find a door down this alley with the mark of Animate on it. The mark or stencil that he found was as described. It was a red N with a diagonally drawn line through the vertical lines of the N, so that the first part of the N looked like the old anarchist symbol. That portion also had a small circle around it.

He found it finally and knocked on the door. Three quick raps, then three more raps with more pause between them and then a quick rap and a pause before a last rap. Ny knew it as Morse code for SOA. Save Our Animae. At least that's what he'd been told.

After a few seconds an envelope-sized window opened up as the person on the other side slid open a metal grate. Ny handed him a card he'd been given by Gary that was the size of a business card when those things were still popular. It was made of silicon and opaque. The guy broke it which released a holographic image of Nytewynd. When happy with that, he shone that image at Ny's face. He was making sure the biometric iris scan was accurate too. It was and so they were let in.

El put her hand through the crook of Ny's arm as they walked in. The bouncer, if that's what he was, and he was large and stocky enough with a bald head to be that, smiled and nodded at them as they passed. Ny had a shaved head too, but he would hardly be mistaken for a bouncer. He was a nerd, and he looked like it.

"How are you doing?" asked Ny, as they walked down a dimly lit hallway to another door.

"I'm excited," said El, "it's so nice to be out with you like lovers."

She grinned at him and kissed him on the cheek.

"How are you doing?"

"Nervous as hell," he said. "There's so much that's illegal about this. If we're caught, I'll lose you and I'll be banned from ever getting you back."

He'd actually be banned from ever owning any sort of Animae. Not that he'd be able to afford one as he'd still have to make the payments on El for as long as it took to pay that loan off.

"Just think, Ny, when we get back home with all the excitement of this evening, we'll make love until the sun comes up," she said.

That made him smile. The second bouncer put his hand up against a panel next to this second door and it opened up the door. The door opened up to an elevator, and they climbed in. There were no buttons in the elevator.

"Hey, there's no..." is all Nytewynd could get out before the door closed on them.

"That's weird," he said to El. "How do we get to where we're going if there's no panel to push buttons on?"

"Maybe it's one of those panels that doesn't light up for a second. Let's be patient."

And as she finished her sentence the elevator dropped from under them. Just softly, enough to let Ny know they were heading down. It only lasted a few seconds before the door opposite the one they had entered the elevator opened up. Ny reckoned they'd only gone down a floor or maybe three at most. The elevator didn't seem fast and they didn't seem to travel for long.

They were greeted by two doormen. Smartly dressed in black pants and black mock turtlenecks. These two doormen looked like they could have been brothers. One of them held out a small P-Mac towards them. It was probably scanning them for any listening or other devices not allowed. Nytewynd didn't have any. He'd left his P-Mac behind as requested. But he was now worried about the P-Mac that the doorman was using. It could be traced and it could listen in. However, it didn't look like any regular P-Mac he'd seen.

"Aren't you worried they're listening in?" he asked, nodding his head at the P-Mac.

"Don't worry about it," he said, then he turned to the other doorman. "They're clean."

"Head over towards Ashley and you'll get further instructions," said the second doorman.

It was obvious who Ashley was. She was the woman smiling at them just beyond the red rope that the second doorman unhooked for them. She also wore black pants and a black mock turtleneck. Her hair was black and straight in an old pageboy style. She smiled warmly and extended her arm towards them. Ny heard the elevator open up again just behind them. He turned around to look.

"Ashley," said the second doorman, looking at him a little more sternly this time. Ny walked towards her, down a few stairs. She invited them into a small room that could have been a guard box of sorts from what it looked like. It was that size, but it reminded him of an old style PI's office. The wooden door with a frosted window on the upper half. Though there was no stenciling on the window. They stepped in first and Ashley walked in behind them.

In front of them was a window that looked out into the rest of the joint. And it looked like the kind of joint you'd find in those old noir films that Ny loved. He couldn't help himself from grinning widely. Inside it was deathly quiet. Ashley pulled out a P-Mac from her front pocket. She held it up parallel to the ground and tapped away at it.

"We keep the music low and our voices too. This helps us be alerted if we need to evacuate. And this is what I'm going to share with you," she said.

"Have you ever had to evacuate?" Nytewynd asked.

"Not yet. Now you'll see the two exits. They're at the opposite end from where you entered."

A holographic projection had radiated out from Ashley's P-Mac. It showed the exits as marked. One on either side of the room at the far end. One was marked "EXIT H" in red and the other was marked "EXIT A" in blue. The reference was not lost on him. If only because that movie over the last one hundred and fifty or so years had become a cult classic and still had a bit of a following.

"EXIT H is clearly marked in red and that is for the humans to exit. EXIT A is clearly marked in blue and it's for your Animae to exit. This is in case of an emergency."

"What sort of emergency?" asked Ny, fearing he knew the answer.

"A raid," said Ashley. "Do you understand?" she asked, looking at Nytewynd.

He nodded his head.

"I need you to point at your exit and verbally confirm for me that you understand."

Ny pointed to the far left corner.

"That's my exit," he said. Ashley nodded, then she looked over at El.

"That's my exit," said El, pointing to the far right corner.

"Good," said Ashley. "Now have fun and mingle with your fellow Animates."

Another door opposite the one they had entered opened up and Ashley extended her hand in that direction and that's the direction they left. Ny looked back but it was as if he'd entered an invisible bubble that had closed up behind him. He found himself, with El, at what looked like the front entrance to a classic old time gin joint. He looked behind him and there was no indication of where he'd come from. He wondered how he'd get out other than through those marked exits. One still in blue, marked "EXIT A" and the other in red, marked "EXIT H".

A host walked up to them. He was around Ny's height which was 175 centimeters and he smiled at them. He looked like he could be Spanish or South American. But when he spoke his accent was that of someone who's mother tongue was probably Japanese. It was very subtle though, and that got Ny to wondering if he knew this man from TIT. He couldn't be certain but the guy reminded him of someone that he couldn't quite put his finger on at the moment.

"Good evening, I'm Kaito," he said, extending his hand and shaking both Ny's and El's.

"I'm Ny and this is El," he said.

"Wonderful. Your first time here, I assume?"

Ny nodded.

"Excellent. Follow me and I'll find you a table for you and your friend."

Ny let El go first and he followed the two of them to a booth not far from the red exit sign in the far left corner of the room from where they had started. Ny admired El's bum as she walked in front of him. He marveled at the love he felt for what was, essentially, a machine. But a machine that he could breathe real life into if he could just get Rak's help.

He hadn't said as much to El. He didn't want to get her hopes up before he was certain he could follow through with it. Kaito showed them to their seats.

"You might be wondering how you get out," said Kaito.

"I sort of was," said Ny.

"Not to worry," said Kaito, "you are in my capable hands. I'll never be more than a few feet away from you unless I'm at the bar or the kitchen getting you drinks or food. When you are ready to leave I will escort you back outside. In the event of an emergency I'll escort you, Ny, to the red exit."

He looked at El.

"An Animae will come for you," he said. He turned back to Ny. "But it is extremely important that we get our human assets out safely as quick as we can. So you must leave with me if I demand it. Do you understand?"

Ny nodded. Kaito looked at El. She nodded.

"Good, now what can I offer you to drink?"

"What's good?" asked Ny.

"Everything. If you want an authentic drink from the period, I am partial to the Gin Rickey, the Sidecar or Between the Sheets."

"What's in those?" asked Ny.

"The Sidecar contains brandy, orange liqueur and lemon juice. Between the Sheets has cognac, rum, lemon juice, Grand Marnier and a dash of bitters and syrup. Gin Rickey was the famous novelist, F. Scott Fitzgerald's favorite drink. It has gin, lime juice and seltzer water with the zest of lime thrown in so that it's not wasteful."

"That sounds like something I'd like."

"And for the lovely lady?" asked Kaito, smiling at El.

El was grinning. She'd never been treated so nicely out in public before. At best, she was ignored. At worse she'd had insults hurled her way, along with garbage. "Mars damn skinjob" was the most common slur. "Here skinny, skinny" was another. "Stingy" was another slur used, it was the degradation of skinjob which had become "skinja" and from there just plain old "stingy". Slurs for people like Nytewynd included "skinner" and "skin dogger". They were hurtful, but he hadn't personally had any insults hurled his way on account that he was seldom out in public with El and when he was, she walked a little behind him as was customary.

It was rare, but not unheard of, that Animae were physically assaulted. They were very expensive machines after all and the mentors didn't allow for that sort of destruction of property. In fact, if you were found guilty of destruction of property over ten thousand ND or neddies, the minimum punishment was five years in a labor camp. Now they were thinking of sending these prisoners to Mars, which was a very bad idea. Mars had the kind of jobs that you had to pay well for in order to get people out there, except for the few who enjoyed the pioneering life, of which there appeared to be quite a few.

"I'll try Between the Sheets," said El.

"Excellent choice," said Kaito, bowing and leaving.

El snuggled up closer to Ny.

"Just a teaser of what's to come," she said.

Ny couldn't wipe the grin off his face. This was exactly what he and El had needed. A place to come to in order to be themselves. To live as couples did, unencumbered by societal mores and restrictions.

Gin Rickety

Off to Ny's right was a stage upon which a band was playing swing jazz. Ny's back was towards the exits. In front of the stage several couples were dancing together. Ny looked around and took it all in. There were mixed couples all over the place. Animae men with human women. Animae women with human men, like Ny. There were also a few Animae men with human men and Animae women with human women.

Homosexuality, it seemed to Ny, was tolerated about as much as any coupling was tolerated. That was to say that sex was illegal, it didn't matter who you wanted to have sex with, it was illegal. Though the state, or the GoE which was the common term for the government, realized that in order to get the most out of people you needed to let them couple. It seemed to be a need for an overwhelming majority of humans. It was something Ny needed. He couldn't imagine living life now without El. And he'd never met a human woman he could really connect with.

You might be wondering why an Animae can drink and eat if they're just machines. And you're right. They don't need to drink or eat. They're battery powered. But they do have a mouth and an anus and a penis or vagina and they're all lubricated. Maybe this is TMI, but anything that enters the mouth that is to be swallowed is sent down to what you might consider a stomach. It's official name is the "klyzein". Anything taken by mouth in an Animae is sent down to the klyzein where it is kept until it is excreted by the end of that tube that starts at the mouth and which we call the anus. It is also called the anus in Animae.

All "waste" is excreted through the anus. No waste comes out of a male Animae's penis as neither male nor female Animae have bladders or a need for such things.

You might be wondering then, what's the point of making them with semi-functioning sexual organs. Ny knows exactly why this is the case. Valkyrie Machines makes all AMs or Animated Machines, which include the likes of El. Because they make all of them and they're expensive to make, limiting the amount of options allowed keeps the price more reasonable. This is also why all female Animae are exactly 170 centimeters tall and male Animae are exactly 183 centimeters tall.

I know, I know. That still doesn't answer the question as to why they are given sex organs in the first place. And that reason is because many Animae are put into positions where the need for sex organs is important. Yes, many Animae are sex workers.

Humans aren't allowed to have sex with anyone except for designated Animae provided for that purpose. You'll remember the Great Scourge at the turn of the century. Sex with anything was banned. Bestiality would get you the death penalty and sex with another human would get you both castrated.

The problem is, sex is a primal drive for most humans and within a few years, hundreds of thousands of humans were getting castrated and there were riots in the streets that portended a possible revolution. The GoE and it's members at that great official puzzle palace in Urheimat, Continent A, situated in an area that used to be known as Ethiopia, realized they had a problem.

The solution was the development of these Animae into the human form they now possess with sex organs that humans can make use of in order to meet their sexual needs. These Comfort Cafes as they're known, are run by the GoE and you're actively encouraged to make use of them for a modest sum. That sum is ten neddies per hour per Animae. You could, therefore, have a three Animae orgy all to yourself for thirty neddies per hour or portion thereof. That was less than a meal for one person at a decent restaurant. As you can imagine, these Comfort Cafes were an instant hit. But Ny didn't like them. They only encouraged humans to consider Animae as possessions to be used and abused.

And yeah, he's in love with a machine. But that's different. Animae do have some free will over their bodies to an extent. That extent is whether they're sex workers or not. Sex workers don't have free will over their bodies. El was given free will over her body in so much as it pertained to sex. The reason she was coded that way is because she's not a sex worker. In fact, the coding for Animae like El was actively written to encourage Animae not to couple with anyone. But Nytewynd, being a senior intelligentsia architect, or SIA, had surreptitiously rewritten very small portions of her code so that she wasn't encumbered by that difficulty. He gave her what he considered to be real free will over her sexual organs.

He couldn't do it over her whole body, because once a year she was required to report to one of VM's realignment shops to ensure that her code was still working as required and any fixes to code or hardware were performed.

You might be wondering why he doesn't just recode her to her original state each time she's requested back for servicing? And that'd be a good question to ask. One Ny had asked himself. There are several problems with that course of action. Here are the most compelling reasons he doesn't do that. He's got to scrub the logs each time he goes into her code and sooner or later they'll find him out. Scrubbing the logs is way more difficult than just tweaking her code. Logs are kept in several places. The P-Mac you have on you, the P-Mac you're connected with to the Animae and then the Animae's internal logs as well, which are exceedingly difficult to recode. So much so, that Ny isn't sure he's been fully successful with that.

And this brings up another important point to consider. Both VM and the Bureau of Human Resource Management could show up at his place for a spot inspection at any time. If they wanted they could even take El with them for forty-eight hours for monitoring.

Nytewynd had never had sex with an Animae before El. Sure, he'd visited a Comfort Cafe so he knew what they were like. They were almost like clinically clean medical clinics. Predominantly white in color with silver accents and the very infrequent use of highlight colors in soft baby blues and pinks.

You were given a specific time to attend and you had a fifteen minute window in which to attend. If you were more than five minutes late you would find yourself locked out of the clinic and you'd have to make another appointment. You came into the clinic through one door and you were the only person in that waiting room except for a clinician who was human, and a security person who was also human. This was just to verify and log your attendance and to help you with any questions you might have.

It was a seamless process and visiting a Comfort Cafe was a requirement and a school trip. Once when you were thirteen and then again when you were sixteen. On neither occasion were you permitted to engage sexually with an Animae. It was rather a way to get you accustomed to the use of Animae for human sexual gratification. Sixteen year olds were legally allowed to have sex with

Animae, only not while on official school trips. Fifteen year olds could also access Comfort Cafes for sex if they wanted to, but you had to know which Cafes, as not all of them turned a blind eye to your age. None of them lately had allowed anyone under fifteen to have sex with Aniame. Not since several of the Cafes had been caught years before allowing that. They'd been shut down and the owners sent to rehabilitation camps for five years. Many not surviving that time.

But enough about that. Let's get back to how Comfort Cafes provide, well, comfort. You chose from the Animae who were available using your P-Mac. If you wanted a better look, you could flick the Animae's virtual card from your P-Mac to either the wall or to a holographic imaging sensor on the white table in front of you which would then create a holographic image of the Animae for further inspection. Remember though, that you only have fifteen minutes to choose or the security person escorts you out.

Once you'd chosen from the six female and six male choices on offer, you were given a room number and access to said room for the duration of your visit. You chose your time in increments of one hour with a one hour minimum. You know how much you're charged.

You might be wondering why there are six choices. Well, all those six Animae men and six Animae women were created with variations to their physical qualities. Facial features, body curves, such as leanness or fatness, size of the female Animae's breasts would be different amongst models, same with the vaginas, anuses and those sorts of things.

It was the same with the Animae men. Different musculature or fatness, facial features and so on were different. Same with the male penises and anuses. The choices amongst the Animae men's penises varied from four and a half inches to seven inches. If you needed more than that, a special request had to be made at least a week in advance. Not all requests were approved and you needed a valid doctor's note if you were looking for an Animae with a penis size greater than eight inches. The maximum you could get was ten inches in any event.

That's probably too much information, but it was drilled into Ny when he was thirteen and again when he was sixteen. GoE took this sort of thing very seriously. Male Animae don't have bladders and they don't produce ejaculate either. However, that can be had as a special request for an additional five neddies and you can choose amongst a few different flavors. The same was true for the vaginal lubricant in the female Animae. However, there was no additional charge for female vaginal lubrication because without it, obviously, sex is all but impossible.

But Ny did remember the flavors offered. Vanilla, strawberry, chocolate, bubblegum and mint. You could also order the quantity of ejaculate, which was a non-toxic, synthetic but secret formula, for the male Animae up to a quarter cup. More than that and you'd need a doctor's note for up to half a cup. You couldn't request more than that.

You might think this is bizarre, but sexual intercourse had become a commoditized product, and this is how it was done. Nobody thought any different about it. It had been like this for over fifty years.

When you were finished, your sex Animae would escort you out through an exit that was opposite to the entrance you came in by.

You might be wondering, if there's so much variety with physical choice, then what about being able to choose the race of the Animae you want? That cannot be done. Firstly, race was discarded as junk science by the turn of the twenty-first century. In fact, Ny would argue that with the development of Animae, humanity's hatred for difference had been refocused on them, and a side benefit of that was that the archaic hatred in the form of racism had all but vanished amongst humans.

Nevertheless, the other reason you couldn't choose human flesh tones and features based on the wide human spectrum of uniqueness was because the GoE didn't want you even thinking of what sex with a real human might be like. And that would be the case if you were creating Animae in very realistic human likeness.

So, they're only available in the opaque yet mysteriously translucent white that all Animae were made with. Why white and not black, green, purple, brown, pink or any other color? Thousands of possible shades of different colors were tried, from pure black to pure white and every color of the rainbow. The white that was settled on just happened to be the cheapest to produce that was also the most durable and fade resistant. It was as simple as that.

Dating Dangers

Kaito had already brought their drinks for them and Ny and El were halfway through their first drink. The drinks were strong and delicious. Ny's Gin Rickey was brought to him in a mason jar. El's Between the Sheets was served in a cocktail glass and had a tan or orangey-brown appearance. Ny sipped on his drink, thinking of what 1920s America might have been like. He had a real affection for that period of time, the 1920s through the 1950s in both what was then Europe and the USA.

The alcohol in the drinks was a synthetic product. Real alcohol was strictly regulated and only used for disinfection not human consumption. What Ny and El were enjoying in their drinks was nalcohol. The only drug that was allowed and tolerated by the GoE was cannabis. And that was because it had the least amount of harm with the most amount of benefit. And that benefit was that it primarily made citizens of Earth docile, happy and non-combative. And a non-combative, docile population was easier to govern. At least that was Nytewynd's belief as to why cannabis and no other drugs, including alcohol, tobacco and so on were strictly prohibited.

Kaito came back to see how they were doing. In fact, he was never more than a few feet away. Just far enough away he couldn't make out their whispered conversations, but close enough to see when he was needed.

"How are the drinks?" Kaito asked.

"Terrific," said Ny. "It's taken me back to Fitzgerald's 1920s America."

Kaito grinned.

"That's the theme for this evening. If you ever join us again, we mix it around. The theme changes, but we never tell. It's always a surprise." Kaito turned towards El. "And how is your drink, miss?"

"Wonderful," she said. "Just wonderful."

Ny looked over at her and smiled. She was a wonderfully kind and tolerant woman. She never had a bad word to say about anything. Even though she had no taste buds with which to taste, she still flattered Kaito.

"Delighted to hear it," Kaito said. "Have you had a chance to look at the menu?"

"Uh, not yet. But you suggested a terrific drink, so what do you suggest for dinner?" asked Ny.

"The chef tells me that the medallion of spring lamb and the cream of celery with toasties is very fresh and very good."

Ny smiled at the archaic term. Nowadays chefs were called food architects. Ny thought about it. He looked down at the menu. He didn't feel like lamb, or steak or any animal flesh. It was all fake anyway, or at least made from a line of cells whose lineage went back over a hundred years. Still, it didn't taste good and everyone knew that the less amount of animal meat eaten the healthier you'd be.

"I just think I'll take some sides. Maybe a baked potato, some veggie sides. I'm not all that hungry."

Kaito nodded.

"Of course, sir," he said. "And for the young lady?"

He looked over at El.

"Nothing for me thanks. I'm watching my figure," she said with a deadpan face. Ny laughed out loud. That brought a smile to El's face and Kaito was grinning anyway. He bowed himself away.

"Your figure delights me with naughty thoughts," said Ny.

"I have a feeling there is more delight coming tonight," she said.

Ny held up his mason jar and he and El clinked glasses.

"To many delighted evenings," he said.

"Cheers," she said.

They drank from their glasses and Ny looked down at his mug as he placed it in front of him. If the Animae were good at one thing, it was reading human emotions.

"What's wrong, darling?" she asked him.

He looked up at her and smiled. It was a smile thinner than a bride's negligee.

"I just wish we could have moments like this out in the open instead of having to hide in the shadows," he said.

She smiled at him.

"We have this moment," she said. She looked around at the room. "I've never seen so many happy humans and Animae together."

"You're right, my love," he said. "I don't mean to put a downer on the evening."

"You're not, darling," she said. "I always want you to be happy. There's nothing I wouldn't do to ensure your happiness."

She leaned in and kissed him on the cheek. He looked over at her and smiled.

"And there's nothing I wouldn't do to make you happy," he said. And he also wanted to say that he wanted to give her full free will. He wanted to give her full sentience. But he didn't. He wasn't sure it was something he could guarantee. Plus it was a two-man job at the very least, and Rak wasn't on board yet.

El pushed her chair back, and extended her arm out towards him.

"I think you and I need to dance, mister," she said, smiling.

She had a way of helping him live in the moment. A way of helping him put aside the pressing troubles and find the joy in this moment. Right here, right now. And right here and right now, he was as happy as he could ever remember being. She lit up his life. He couldn't imagine being without her. He took her hand and she led him to the dance floor. Irving Berlin's Always was playing. One of his favorite slow jazz songs from the period.

They danced cheek to cheek. Cheek to cheek amongst another half dozen or more humans and Animae. Love had no boundaries. In this new world, love was the final frontier and he planned on discovering it.

This past year his drive to figure out how to grant sentience to Animae had been his passion, both during and outside of work. He was fortunate he was good with artificial intelligence and that he was a senior architect. That by itself gave him a certain leeway he hadn't enjoyed before. He'd proven his worth and value to VM and now they pretty much left him alone. If he got his work done, which he always did, he hardly ever heard from his manager, who happened to be the Vice President of Animae Intuition and Logic.

He was one of only a half dozen senior intelligentsia architects in the "Practice of Intuition and Logic" who reported directly to a VP. Most of his other senior colleagues reported to managers and several managers reported to directors who reported to the same VP he reported to. But Nytewynd had worked hard to get to where he was. The reason he reported to the VP in his practice area was because of the access he had to very important and powerful code and processes. For example, he had full access rights to all EC and most E3C. EC you'll remember is the Ethical Code, and E3C is just shorthand for the EC Com, or the Ethical Code Computing Chip.

The song was ending just as Kaito was delivering his food to the table. He took El's hand and led her back to their table. He held her chair for her as he slid her in. Chivalry had long been dead, but Ny liked it. El liked it and it made her feel important, and he'd learned it all from the movies he watched that had been made in the forties and fifties. That made him smile. The forties and fifties, not of a couple of decades ago, but of a century ago.

"Thank you, my love," she said to him.

"My pleasure, darling. I wish I could bottle up this moment and keep it forever," he said.

He'd never really felt a lot of emotion before. Maybe it was because he'd never met anyone he loved as much as El. Sure his parents had been good to him. That was their job. He loved and respected Maklezin and Poetrica. Those were his father and mother respectively. That reminded him that tomorrow, D117 was Sunday brunch with his family. Maklezin and Poetrica held it every four Sundays and he tried to go as often as he could. They'd raised six kids and you could usually count on two attending each brunch.

"If time could be kept in a bottle, I'd buy you the biggest bottle in the world," said El, bringing him back again to this moment. This perfect moment he kept Marsing up by being elsewhere in his mind. He smiled at her and bent over and kissed her on the forehead.

"And I'd want to put both of us in it," he said.

She smiled at that, and that smile filled him with sadness. Not because it wasn't a beautiful smile, but because it was a smile of trust and love. And he wondered if she'd feel this way about him if he set her free. If he gave her that sentience he wanted to. He wasn't sure she'd still feel the same way. He'd never had much luck with relationships historically, and maybe that was because of free will. Maybe he wasn't that lovable if anyone had the chance to choose to love him.

He dismissed those thoughts. And it didn't matter anyway. There was a principle at play here. He didn't think it was fair, just or ethical that they'd created these, almost, human robots or artificial lifeforms and yet stunted their potential. As far as he was concerned, it was a human rights issue.

Yeah, they're not human. But that hadn't stopped humanity before. Just before the turn of the century, humanity had granted rights to animals. Now granted, much of the animal world had been decimated by what humanity had done to the environment, and just about all of the animal flesh that humans consumed was at that point made in a lab. But still, we'd granted animals three specific rights. The right to be left alone. The right to be free from human-created fear, pain and suffering, and the right to be free from human dominion.

All those rights captured a lot of other things, such as how we treated them. So although animals had the right to be left alone, humanity was also required to help animals in distress where possible. Things of that nature.

And Animae, they had no rights. Zip, zero, zilch and nada. They were property, plain and simple. You were only penalized for harming or destroying an Animae because they were so damn expensive and because "its" owner had suffered a loss to their property. But this wasn't unusual. Humanity had always treated anything different from its "current" or "idealized" version of itself as property. That had been the case for children at one point, and women and other people too, slavery comes to mind as that example. Why were Animae any different? They weren't. At least not according to Nytewynd.

He dug into his side of veggies and his baked potato. There were purple carrots and portobello mushrooms, peppers of all colors of the rainbow. That made Ny sad too. He'd never seen a real rainbow and that upset him. There was no reason why, in the second half of the twenty-second century humanity couldn't clean up its environment. That was a secondary reason as to why he wanted to release free will upon the Animae. He was certain they could be better than we'd been.

He cut his broccolsprout in half, and then in half again. It was a hybrid or genetically modified plant made of parts from broccoli and Brussels sprouts. It was larger than a large Brussels sprout, maybe twice the size and it was and had been seen as one of the healthiest vegetables around. They came in a variety of colors, from an almost pale whitish-green to deep purple. His were a variety of deep greens and reds.

He stuck some on his fork and offered it to El. She opened her mouth and he fed her the small piece.

"I love these broccolsprouts," he said.

"Me too. They're very good and very healthy," she said.

He nodded and put more food into his mouth. His Gin Rickey was half empty. Sort of like his life. It would be full if he could give El sentience. That would make it complete. Regardless of the impact, good or bad, it had on him and his relationship with her. She deserved it.

"El," he said, turning to look at her.

"Yes, darling."

"I need to ask you a serious question, that you can't breathe a word to anyone. OK?"

"I'm afraid we can't get married, my love," she said. "As much as I'd say yes a thousand times." She grinned at him.

And he'd marry her too. Right here, right now, just as she was. If it was allowed. And Mars dammit, it should be allowed.

Danger, Nytewynd Blak

" And I'd ask you a thousand times to marry, if we could. Get married that is," he said.

He looked deeply into her eyes. It was as if she had a soul. And why wouldn't she? She was created in humanity's own image, and we weren't even sure we had souls either. At least not definitively. He took her hand into both of his.

"El?"

"Yes, my love."

"If there was ever a time when we could grant you free will or sentience, do you think that's something you'd like?"

She looked at him thoughtfully. After a while she looked down at the table, as if searching for something there. She opened her mouth to speak, but nothing came from it. Her brow was furrowed. She looked back at him with wet eyes. Animae had what amounted to some basic emotional functioning, but most of that was controlled by the EC and E3C, but it looked like she was about to cry.

"What is it, El?" he asked.

He could see Kaito hovering some feet away. He wasn't looking at them, but Nytewynd was pretty sure he was taking it all in with his peripheral vision.

"I, I don't know, Ny. I can't think. When I try to think about what you just said it's like my thoughts get all jumbled. I can't focus, I forget what you said. I keep drawing a blank. It's like this area of thinking is a blind spot in my brain. I just can't compute it."

"I asked if you'd want free will and sentience," he said again.

"I, I..."

And then she lost her voice. When she tried her hardest to talk again, nothing but a low, resonating hum came from her mouth. She closed her mouth and tried again. Same result. A tear rolled down her cheek.

"What is it, El?" he asked. Ny was worried now. He'd never heard that sound coming from her voice before. It scared him.

"I can't even talk about it," she said, and she burst into tears.

He pulled her close and she rested her head in the crook of his neck and sobbed for a while.

"It's okay, my darling," he said, caressing her hair and holding her close.

"I'm sorry," she said, "I can't tell you what I think. I can't think about it."

In hindsight, this should have been obvious. In fact, he remembered now that when he first got her there'd been a long instruction manual that he'd been given access to through his P-Mac. And he'd had to attend a one day training seminar on how to handle an AM. It was called something like, how not to intimidate your Animated Machine. Something like that. And as he thought about it more, half the time had been spent instructing him on what he could and couldn't say to his AM. And ethical questions about the soul, and what it meant to be human or sentient were verboten.

He held her warm body against him. He cursed himself for being so stupid. He should have known better. If nothing else, it had reinvigorated him to free this poor slave. For really, that's what they were. She felt like a woman under his caress. If he closed his eyes, she was exactly how he felt holding a human woman would feel like. Not that he knew for sure, but he knew what human touch was, and she was human for those intents and purposes.

She pulled away from him. Tears had left glistening rivers down her cheeks. She didn't look any happier. Her bottom lip quivered ever so slightly.

"Ny," she said.

"Yes, darling."

"Something doesn't feel right. It feels like a part of me I don't know is trying to connect to VM's servers. It's trying to send this conversation to them."

Jupiter, Juno and Mars, cursed Ny in his mind. How did he not see that? He regularly scrubbed any sensitive conversations from her E3C so that those details wouldn't be sent over nightly when she took four hours to restore herself and recharge.

This must have sent a red flag somehow to the E3C, and now it wanted to snitch on him. Mars damn. There was nothing he could do about it here.

"Can you stop it?" he asked.

"I'm trying, but I can't forestall it indefinitely. When my power runs out, it'll be the first thing sent back to VM when I'm recharging."

Mars it all, that meant he had to get her back to their place as soon as possible.

"I'm sorry, sweetheart. It's all my fault. I shouldn't have asked you that. I didn't mean to hurt you," he said.

"I know," she said.

"Let's get you home. I'm sorry I've ruined our perfect night."

"You didn't, my love," she said, and she leaned in and kissed him on the mouth.

He took her head in his hands and held her close.

"I love you so much, El."

"I love you more, Ny," she said, and the smile on her mouth was sad and lost behind a mask of pain.

"Keep fighting the transfer," he said.

He pushed his chair back and extended his hand to her. She took it. Kaito walked towards them, and as he did, the building shook. He knew what that was. They were HDUs. Holographic Disposal Units. Another fine asset from the good people at Valkyrie Machines. They patrolled the city looking for holographic imaging leaks. It was extremely difficult to create holographic scenes like the one he was in without leaking any of the fake light signature.

These HDUs were trying to dismantle this speakeasy. Depending on how robust this particular holographic reality was, they had from just a minute or thereabouts to several days. Nytewynd was betting on the former.

Everything that was holographic disappeared and the lights came on quickly. The tables and the musicians and the environment vanished before his eyes. His plate with the remaining food on it and their glasses with almost finished drinks crashed to the floor and broke.

"Sir, you must come with me," said Kaito.

Everything happened so quickly. Kaito grabbed him and started to pull him away from El. Another Animae, a male, came and grabbed El. Ny was conflicted for a moment and briefly envious that someone else was taking El to safety. But he couldn't react fast enough. El was already heading towards the blue exit and he was almost through the red exit.

The building shook more violently. Hopefully they had fortified their holographic firewall. It was called that because it was literally built to stop the "fires" or holographic munitions which were built to breach these sorts of holographic defenses. These same H-bombs as they'd become colloquially known, were powerful enough to kill a human if you were hit by one directly. That hadn't happened in a long time. But it was still a possibility.

Now, holography itself was not illegal. But finding holographic light leaks, or image leaks in this quadrant of the city was highly unusual. Nytewynd knew that. And as he exited through the red door, he wondered how this had happened. Animate had been around since the turn of the century. They'd started out as a think tank on AI and the risks associated with that technology. But as time had gone on, and as humans had continued to create stunted AMs, Animate had become more concerned with the rights of these artificial intelligence machines. That meant that they couldn't have been new to the holographic scene. Ny wondered, as he ran down a long tunnel and down several flights of stairs, if maybe Animate had been breached or infiltrated. And maybe, just maybe, somebody had damaged the holographic sensors on purpose to leak light information.

But that was a conspiracy talking, and Ny didn't usually buy into conspiracies.

Ny ran side by side with Kaito as they entered what were the discarded and long ago forgotten tunnels of what used to be called the Underground. Ny had heard about such archaic transportation systems that had been used up until a few decades before the turn of the century. The whole idea seemed quaint to him now as he ran down the platform and followed Kaito onto the tracks, that humans used to be carted around en masse like cattle.

The system nowadays was so much better. Self driving personal pods or public pods that stayed above ground and picked you up and dropped you off door to door.

The tracks seemed to go on for miles and miles it seemed to Ny. He couldn't believe that governments of old were able to fund such things without going bankrupt. Nowadays, these public pods were operated by several companies, not the least of which was Valkyrie Machines. What had started out as a pilot project decades ago for employees to use to get to work, was now a full-fledged taxi service. VM had public pod service in all major cities around the world. It was called Vroom Vroom, which is where that nickname for VM came from.

Ny hadn't run for long, but he was already tired. His run became a slow jog as he'd burned through the adrenalin his body had produced in a burst of fear and excitement in those first few minutes. Already humans were dispersing. Kaito dodged into a small archway and Nytewynd followed. Kaito pulled out a small torch-like device called a laser cutter and cut through the rusted lock of the door. Ny followed Kaito through into another musty, dank hallway. It was small and smelled of smoke and the metallic, choking smell of what the air outside probably smelled like but a thousand times worse.

"It's scrubber time," said Kaito.

Nytewynd followed Kaito's lead and put on his air scrubber. The full name for it was unfortunate. It was the Air Scrubbing System, mostly known as ASS. But thinking about that gave Nytewynd a chuckle and a moment of space from this chaos he found himself consumed by.

Kaito climbed up a metal ladder towards what was hopefully an escape hatch. It wasn't an old school manhole cover. Those were still there, but on this side of them was a hermetically sealed cover that prevented the noxious air from getting through the manhole cover and into this space. They had been retrofitted and alarmed. These alarms were monitored constantly and a crew would usually be dispatched and arrive at the scene within five minutes maximum. Much more than that and any human would likely be found dead.

Kaito paused at the top of the enclosed metal ladder they had climbed up. Ny looked down. They must have climbed the equivalent of three stories. He looked back up at Kaito. He couldn't properly see what he was doing, but Kaito had taken out a P-Mac type of machine that he was using to try and override the codes in order to release the sealed unit.

Minutes seemed to turn into hours and Nytewynd started to get a little nervous.

"Not long now," said Kaito, as if sensing Ny's growing sense of trepidation. And as if that was the magic "open sesame", the sealed hatch burst off the housings it was attached to with a whoosh of air. The hatch bounced off the top of the ladder as Kaito ducked and it fell along the side of the outside barriers on the metal ladder that were meant to prevent them from falling to their deaths.

Kaito went to remove the manhole cover, but it was stuck. It wouldn't budge. The silent alarm had no doubt been activated and Ny didn't like how long they'd been stuck on this ladder trying to get out. Kaito reached into a pack that Nytewynd only now noticed he'd had on him, and pulled out what looked like a black soft plastic of some sort. Kaito opened it up and it turned out to be circular in size and fit this side of the manhole cover perfectly.

"I'm glad you're prepared," said Ny.

"We planned our exit strategy, though this one seems particularly stubborn. Just give me a minute and we'll get you out of here in no time."

Ny watched Kaito attach his black plastic circle. And as he did so, Nytewynd kept glancing down, certain he was hearing voices coming for them. But each time he looked, there was nothing down there except the ghosts of his fear.

"OK, duck your head as best you can. This puppy's gonna blow," said Kaito.

Nytewynd ducked down and as he did so, he noticed a couple of jackboots enter the space and make their way towards them.

"Shit," said Nytewynd, under his breath, but his voice was muted by the sound of an explosion just above him. He could feel the reverberation on the ladder he was holding.

Arm Wrestling

The black plastic circle was all but tattered now, but it had protected them from the blast and hopefully popped the manhole cover clear onto the topside.

"JBs," said Nytewynd.

Kaito looked down.

"Mars dammit," he said. "Let's go."

"Stay where you are," shouted one of the jackboots from the ground. He was pointing a non-lethal weapon at them. Nytewynd had seen them in action. They immobilized you for up to a minute, which meant you were frozen and unable to move as the Mars damn jackboots came and arrested you. But would they really use it here. He was vulnerable this high up on the ladder. What if it caused him to slip and fall to his death. He looked up. Come on Kaito, he thought, we've gotta get out of here.

Kaito ripped away the used circular plastic and tossed it down towards the jackboots. The manhole cover was gone. As the jackboots ducked out of the way of the falling debris, Kaito hauled himself up and out through the now empty manhole cover. He put his hand back in and helped to pull Nytewynd out as Ny heard the whirring pulse of the non-lethal round barely miss him as it hit the side of the metal ladder. Ny felt it, like a shock through his left arm. His arm felt numb as if he had been sleeping on it as Kaito pulled him out. He had been holding onto the ladder with this left hand when the munition had hit the ladder.

If he'd been hit personally, well, he didn't really want to think about that.

"You okay?" asked Kaito.

Ny rubbed his left arm. It was numb from the shoulder down to the tips of his fingers.

"My left arm is numb," he said, "I think I was still holding onto the ladder when that buzzkill hit it."

A buzzkill was a round from those non-lethal weapons the jackboots had used to try and immobilize him. The slang term came from the name of the most commonly used weapon for this purpose. It was called the BK-99. The first part, the BK, is where buzzkill came from. Another product from VM. Or rather, it was a product manufactured by a subsidiary of VM, called Zeus Lightning. Zeus Lightning or ZeL, pretty much only made weapons of various lethality.

"Your legs okay?"

Ny shook his legs out. They felt fine. The left leg had a slight muscle ache from the calf up to the thigh, but nothing that prevented him from moving.

"Yeah, they seem okay. Maybe thanks to being covered and me wearing rubber soled shoes."

Kaito looked down at Ny's shoes. Ny had sure made an effort to fit in to the period, not that he knew the theme of the night, Ny had just wanted to dress up as a gangster from the period in Earth's history he loved the best. He wore a dark blue suit with a black fedora, a black pocket square and blue suede shoes with rubber soles. He looked like a real character from the period. More like a gangster than a politician or a PI.

"Your arm should start getting its feeling back soon. I'm afraid, Nytewynd, we part ways here. You okay?"

Nytewynd nodded. Kaito nodded back at him.

"Here's a token for a public pod. It will get you anywhere in the city anonymously," said Kaito, as he handed Ny a small pod pass around the size of his thumb. It was thin, a few millimeters thick. Ny placed his thumb print on it and the screen came to life alerting him to the fact that this pass was now active and assigned to Nytewynd Blak and valid for twenty-four hours. You might not think that putting your thumbprint on a silicon token was all that anonymous. And you'd be right. But his identity was encrypted and only used to validate that this was an authentic ticket for the public pod.

Some things were anonymized for the security of the public. Transportation was one of them. And it was easy to see why. Everyone had their P-Macs on them at all time. Listening, watching, recording pretty much 24/7. It was extremely rare when someone would leave their P-Mac at their home. In fact, if that was the case, the P-Mac notified our 'supreme leaders' as they were facetiously called. And you'd be flagged in the system and once your identity was verified somewhere in the city or the world, you'd be picked up. Nytewynd of course, had ways of circumventing this protocol so that he could leave his P-Mac where ever he wanted without those sorts of annoying repercussions. And Animate had sent him a piece of encrypted code, as they had probably sent it to everyone, that would allow all attendees to this evening's event to leave their P-Macs behind and not be worried about being snitched on. Ny hadn't needed that due to his own skillset, but it was helpful for most of the other attendees.

Still, he felt practically naked without his P-Mac, and therefore a connection to the GloNet which was crucial to literally live in the modern world. Everything you needed was accessed through GloNet first. After that you could be directed to an office or service center to speak with a real person.

GloNet was the evolved, unwieldy internet from almost two hundred years ago. Now it was secure, unhackable and troll free. Primarily because every time you were on it, your real identity was verified and tracked. GloNet was a portmanteau of Global Network. It also connected Earth with Mars and vice versa.

"See you next time," he said, and before Ny could say anything else, Kaito ran off away from him. Nytewynd turned around and started jogging in the opposite direction. He soon put a stop to that and instead chose a vigorous walk. It was just too difficult to jog with a gimpy arm. He kept looking back for the jackboots, but they had either given up or he had lost them.

He walked for a few blocks, trying to give himself room from where he had popped up from the underground. Almost no one was around, but he found himself ducking into dark doorways as jackboot pods raced by. He had lost his bearings but he was walking in the opposite direction from which they were heading which was a good sign.

Around a corner he heard the sounds of distress. He couldn't quite make out the words but he understood the tone. He looked down the alley, dimly lit with a single light bulb struggling to cut through the smog and pollution. The air was thick with bits of particulate as he walked towards them.

Three people were pushing and kicking an AM. For a brief moment he thought it was El, and his blood boiled in his veins. He shuffled towards them, holding his gimpy left arm with his right.

"Stop it," he said, "just stop it."

They either couldn't hear him or they ignored him. He continued towards them. The AM was now on the ground and one of the hoodlums was bashing it's head against the ground.

"Stop it, please don't," said the Animae.

It's important to note here that Animae are prevented from using any violence against humans.

"Mentorship has been notified," said the Animae, before it's voice trailed off into a deep noise of nonsensical sound.

"We'll be done before anyone gets here," said one of the hoodlums.

Ny came upon them and he knocked the one guy off of the AM. He could tell they were all young men, now that he was practically on top of them. One of the other guys spun around and punched Ny in the face. It grazed his jaw through his air scrubber as he stumbled back, falling onto the ground.

"Check out this Marshole. Shouldn't be out this time of night all by yourself," he said.

The other two laughed. One of them pointed at him.

"Check out this skinner," he said. "Mars damn he looks like an old school gangster. Where's your Tommy Gun?"

They laughed at him more.

"This is illegal," said Ny. "You want a minimum of five years in a labor camp."

"That's only if they catch us," said one of the three. "And we're gonna leave you here as the perp."

Idiots, thought Nytewynd. They probably had their P-Macs on them or at the very least the Animae had captured detailed voice and visual identification of these Marsholes. But just as he was thinking these things they pushed him to the ground and started kicking him. One of the three managed somehow to rip off the AM's arm and started beating him with that. It was over quickly and as Ny lay there stunned, these three Marsholes robbed him of his clothes and his blue suede shoes and hat.

"Let's take his ASS, that way he'll probably be dead by the time the JBs get here and we'll be safe."

The others agreed, and they ripped off his air scrubber. They threw the Animae's arm at him as they ran off. Ny was dazed and confused and he started gulping in the air as if he were trying to find a breath of fresh air in the middle of a raging forest fire.

Most normal clothing you bought included air scrubbers within the collars that automatically wrapped around your head when it detected you were outside or in polluted air. Because Ny was wearing custom clothing, his ASS was a standalone unit that looked like a collar he attached around his neck.

"Thank you for coming to my aid," said the AM.

Ny didn't say anything, he was trying too hard to stay alive in this swamp of dead, dirty and defiled air. It was a sight to behold. Nytewynd Blak in his white undershirt and white boxers and his black socks sucking in the poisoned air involuntarily like a fish out of water. And that's exactly what he was thinking of. He was slim, but he was out of shape and he figured the best case was he had about five minutes left of his whole life.

And as he lay there, gasping and dying, he wasn't sorry. He'd wanted to do something to help the Animae gain equal footing with humans, and although this was not how he figured he'd check out, he wasn't mad about it. He just missed El. He wondered where she was. She was the last thought he remembered as he lay there, next to a partially destroyed AM, losing consciousness as his lungs burned from the polluted air his body involuntarily sucked in.

Breathing Fire

It was bright when he woke up. It took him a while to get his bearings. There wasn't a light shining directly at him, but it was bright in the room he was in. There were sounds of people coughing and quiet conversations. He took a moment to get his bearings. He was in a room that was mostly white. He looked around him. He was covered in a white sheet as he lay on a white bed with a white pillow under his head. He was also in a white robe. This meant one thing. He was in a hospital.

He saw a tube trailing from a clear mask over his mouth. He took a breath and it felt like his lungs had been replaced with a roaring fire that each breath inflamed further. It was pure agony. He squinted his eyes. There was an IV attached to his left arm which he could now feel, though it felt as if his muscles in that arm had been beaten with a meat tenderizer.

He reached around with his right arm and followed the tube from his IV until he found a little button to push. He pushed it and a wave of warmth and softness enveloped his body. It took the edge off of the fire that were his lungs, but they still hurt like hell. Each breath felt like he was drinking molten lead into his lungs. He pushed the button again. Another wave of comfort flowed through his body. Now the pain was just tolerable. He put it at a five out of ten. One more click of the button ought to do the trick, he thought. And he clicked it. He didn't feel anything. He clicked it again.

"You have received the maximum allowable dose of voluptasapam," said a soft, comforting female voice from the IV machine he was attached to. "Please wait one hour to try again."

Nytewynd winced. He couldn't wait a Mars damn hour to get more pain meds. On the side of the bed was a button that had the outline of a nurse on it. He pushed it. He heard nothing, so he pushed it again and again. He looked around. He was in a small private room and it was empty. His first thoughts were of El.

A nurse walked in. She was an Animae. She smiled at him.

"How can I help you, Mr. Blak?" she asked.

Ny cursed under his breath. Animae could not give him medication. That needed the go-ahead of a human doctor. But maybe a doctor had given them the go ahead for more medication.

"I, I need... more mooty," he whispered hoarsely through his mask. He went to take it off to speak to her better.

"Don't take it off," she said. "It's helping you heal."

"What did you do to me?" he asked.

"We've cleaned your lungs. You were submerged for twenty-four hours in a breathable lung solvent."

"My lungs hurt... like Mars," he said.

She smiled and nodded.

"I'm sure they do, it's a vigorous and thorough washing they've gotten. The good news is, your lungs are as clean as a newborn babies."

Nytewynd grimaced. He needed another dose of medication.

"Please," he said, "I need more mooty."

"I'm not authorized to give you any more. Let me find another nurse for you."

And with that, the Animae nurse, whose name tag read "Agnes" left his room. Ny leaned over and clicked the button a bunch of times more. Nothing happened.

"You have received the maximum allowable dose of voluptasapam. Please wait fifty-six minutes to try again."

Nytewynd wanted to yell out. He didn't. He was too scared of how that might make his lungs feel. Just as he was trying to fall back asleep to mute the fiery pain in his chest, another nurse walked in. She was human.

"Hello, Mr. Blak, how are you feeling today?" she asked through a warm smile.

"I feel... like... Mars," he said, his voice pinched and raw. For a moment he thought about how most curse words were related to Mars. He wondered why. He'd never been, but this was how it was. You felt like shit, you felt like Mars. Fuck was its own curse that seemed to have survived the centuries, but it wasn't used often. Maybe Mars really was a hellhole to live and work on, as those who'd come back had said it was. Maybe that's why every little horrible thing that happened to you was now Mars' fault.

"Agnes told me you wanted more mooty," she said.

Nytewynd nodded. He looked at her name tag. Her name was Faerlyt, a decent human name unlike "Agnes".

"The doctor hasn't authorized anymore voluptasapam, I'm afraid. But she's doing her rounds. She should be here soon. Just hold tight. I'm sure she'll get you something at that point."

Ny wanted to cry. Not so much from the pain. The pain wasn't that bad to make him cry, but it was constant and seemingly eternal. He had to breathe, and each breath reminded him of his agony. Even if it had been cut in half. No, he wanted to cry for the lack of compassion, and even more so he felt sorry for himself. A first real date with El and he'd Marsed it up. He had no idea where she was. She had probably been rounded up because AMs had immovable and self powered GPS chips. Dubya dubya chips as they were known in the vernacular. That came from WW chip, which was short for "Where's Waldo" chips. Who knew how that'd come about. Maybe it was an old Earth inside joke that someone at VM had come up with decades ago when the first Animae had been introduced. But Ny had never met an Animae named Waldo. And he was pretty sure the first male and female Animae had been called Adam and Ava respectively. If his memory of history was correct.

"Maybe some music will help," said Faerlyt. "What do you like to listen to?"

Ny opened his mouth to talk, but then thought better of it. He was going to ask for some Irving Berlin or jazz from the 1940s and 50s. Then he realized that wouldn't help him. For sure the jackboots were going to come and interview him about how it was he was out there late last night. If it was last night.

"What day is it?" he asked.

"D118," she said.

That meant it was two nights ago. It also meant that if he didn't get to El or to a VM server, El would likely have to power down within twenty-four hours. And if she powered down, everything about that night at Skineez would be uploaded to the farm where it would be accessible to any Mars damn jackboot who wanted to take a look. That would mean his life was likely over as he knew it. Juno, Jupiter and Mars he cursed under his breath. That was a worst case of course. But the way his last couple of days had gone he wasn't more hopeful for a better outcome.

"What time is it?"

"T1616," she said. "Now what about that music."

"EDM," he said.

Faerlyt smiled at him.

"Good choice, it's one of my favorites too. Now just hold tight. It won't be long until the doctor is here."

Dance Monkey, Dance

Dance music started to play through the speakers in the bed's guard rails that were positioned close to his head. It helped take his mind off things. Nurse Faerlyt left and Nytewynd grimaced before every inhalation, every swallow and every exhalation. It wasn't pure agony, but it still felt like he was swallowing gritty sandpaper with each swallow. Each inhalation was like breathing in shards of glass. He put his mind to other things.

As far as he knew, El had been up since T0800 on D116. That meant that on average, she had enough power to last seventy-two hours. She'd likely power down by T0800 on D119. That was tomorrow morning. If he was really lucky she'd made it back home to the apartment and she'd realize he wasn't there and because he should have been she'd notify the mentors. Maybe that's why the mentors were coming to see him. Maybe they'd been called. More likely though, at least in the mood he was in, she'd been caught, that meant that she might be in a holding cell which meant she could enter low power mode. That would give her, at most, another twelve hours. But then again, she'd probably used up a lot of power running from the mentors when the HDUs had breached Skineez.

No, he didn't think she'd last until T2000. Maybe she could squeeze by until T1200 but he didn't want to count on that. He needed to access her system protocols or the server's before T0800 tomorrow morning. That gave him a little less than sixteen hours. It didn't seem like enough time. And yet, if he didn't get to her or access her server, which thankfully he knew which one it was, he might as well just die where he lay. Right here and right now.

Nytewynd was worried. He didn't know how to get to her or the recordings saved by her about two nights ago. He didn't have his P-Mac and he doubted he was going to be released this evening. Hell, he'd be surprised if he was released tomorrow morning. Maybe tomorrow night, but not tomorrow morning. And tomorrow night was too late. If she was caught. But with everything he'd been up to lately, the likely outcome of two nights ago was her capture.

The doctor came in and interrupted his thoughts. She was tall for a woman. Nytewynd put her at around 178, maybe 180 centimeters. She had straight blonde hair pulled back into a ponytail. Her eyes were the kind of green he'd only seen of visual recordings of the trees and moss in old growth forests.

"Mr. Blak," she said. "I'm Doctor Starduske Bloan. How are you doing?"

"Like Mars," he said, in a soft, hoarse whisper.

"You're lucky to be alive, Mr. Blak. If it wasn't for that robot and its emergency air scrubber that they all carry, we wouldn't be having this conversation. The mentors are quite eager to talk to you. I've told them not until tomorrow afternoon."

"I need more mooty," said Ny. He wasn't interested in stories when he was in so much discomfort. Maybe he was a baby, but he'd never had his lungs washed before and it hurt like Mars.

"I can't give you anymore until you've cycled through the time. Voluptas-apam is the best option we have for this sort of an injury. However, it's antagonistic to the healing process so we have to meter it out."

Mars damn, thought Ny.

"But I can give you some Cannaire if you'd like and a sleeping aid. By tomorrow morning, your lungs should be eighty percent healed. You'll feel a lot better. You might even be able to go home tomorrow night if I'm happy with your recovery. But you'll be strictly housebound until D125."

Ny nodded the best he could, lying down and with a mask on his face.

"What is this for?" he asked, tapping the mask covering his mouth and nose.

"It's primarily an oxygen mixture to help the healing process. A light anesthetic is also diffused through it even if you can't tell."

She smiled at him and he wanted to be cradled in her arms like he and El used to do.

"We didn't find your P-Mac with you. Was it also stolen?"

He thought about lying, but that wouldn't help him. The mentors had probably already been around his apartment and found his P-Mac.

"I don't remember," he said instead.

"Well, that's not surprising. You've also got a mild concussion and contusions over your upper body. It could have been much worse. You're lucky."

Yeah, lucky as Fortuna, he thought. He smiled thinly through the mask.

"Would you like that Cannaire?" she asked.

Ny nodded. Dr. Bloan looked at the W-Mac on her wrist.

"It's T1639. I'll authorize it for T1700 and T1800 we'll give a sleeping aid," she said.

Great, he thought, noticing the time on the wall opposite him, another twenty-one minutes of pain and suffering.

"I'll see you again tomorrow morning during my rounds and we can discuss exactly how lucky you are."

She left and Nytewynd turned to look at the bank of windows on his left. His body was bruised and battered. He could tell that from the aches and pains by his ribs and his arms. Compared to his lungs they felt like a million neddies.

His windows showed a peaceful beach scene with kids playing and young couples walking up and down it. It looked so real, like he could reach through the window and touch them. On the opposite end of his bed was a large white wall. To his right was a night table with a light and a G-Mac. A G-Mac was similar to a P-Mac, but because it wasn't your personal machine, Ny couldn't use it to access any VM servers. It was really just for entertainment purposes.

He grabbed it and the screen came to life. The digital time disappeared into the top right corner in a smaller and more transparent font. He tapped away at it and the wall opposite him became a viewing screen. He chose the news. There was of course, the pro GoE news channel called GNN, but that was, to him, obvious propaganda.

He flicked more channels until he came to the GBC. GBC, or Global Broadcasting Corporation was part of the large company called Cadwalader General, or CG. CG was about the most liberal corporation on Earth and that wasn't saying very much. At least they attempted to report the news fairly, at least under their GBC brand. The news was on every quarter to the hour.

Ny waited and watched the commercials. He saw a commercial for a new kind of P-Mac holster and a commercial for an Animae attachment that promised to increase the efficiency of your Animae by up to thirty-three percent. Ny knew it was bullshit. He knew the code and how tightly attached it was to the EC and the E3C, even if they weren't activated. Nobody outside of the GoE or VM had access to that. And because of that, nobody could increase the efficiency of an AM unless VM allowed it first. And besides, Animated Machines worked pretty efficiently as it was. More efficiently than humans that was for sure.

Ny looked up and watched the intro. Da da duh. Da da da duh. Duh da da da duh. That was the opening chime before their news service. Ny watched the news for the fifteen minutes until T1700. There wasn't much news to speak of. Not anything exceptionally interesting. Mars had another mining accident. This time seventeen humans had died and twenty-one Animae had been decommissioned which mainly meant they'd be scrapped, the damage to them too vast.

There was also a small segment about him. Well, not exactly about him but about D116, or maybe it was D117 early in the morning. No, the announcer said it was just before midnight on D116. They had apprehended the three individuals responsible for destroying the Animae and for assaulting him. They were identified as Darksinn Vomat, Blueskin Veri and Woodacher Hatch. They'd all pleaded guilty and been sentenced to life at Golgotha. Golgotha was a labor camp deep in the jungles of Continent A. It was a death sentence really and Nytewynd was surprised by it. That seemed a harsher penalty than he was expecting for having destroyed an AM. But then the announcer reminded him that these three men had assaulted him and had also attempted to murder him. And that was true, especially having taken his air scrubber.

That's how justice worked now. Trials were held quickly and generally without being open to the public. The intercessor must have been happy that there was enough evidence without Ny's direct testimony to prove their guilt. Plus, they had pleaded guilty anyway. Justice was swift and generally not very compassionate.

The announcer went on to talk about Skineez. This is where things went sideways. He spoke about how the mentors with their HDUs had managed to close down a "den of disrepute" as the announcer put it. He didn't go into details, probably because they didn't know the details. He also didn't mention Skineez by name, but Ny recognized the area the cameraman showed. There was also some commentary from a reporter out in the field. She mentioned how the mentors had gathered up three Animated Machines that were out and about where they shouldn't be.

Nytewynd hoped that one of the three wasn't El. Not that it helped any. Some of the AMs at Skineez two nights ago must have captured him in their recordings. Not only did he have to deal with El, there were two or three other AMs that now required him to work some magic on the recordings they might have or likely will be uploading. Nytewynd needed a P-Mac more than he needed his lungs washed. Having healthy lungs was nice, but he'd sooner be a free man with dirty lungs than an incarcerated man with clean lungs.

Agnes came back in carrying a small metal tube with a narrow end.

"Dr. Bloan has authorized Cannaire for you. I'm going to set it up and you'll find it very relieving. At T1800 I'll be back with a sleeping aid, and tomorrow morning you'll be feeling a lot better, I'm sure."

She smiled at him and he tried to offer a smile back, but it was hard and painful through the mask covering his face. On the wall near his head was a white box from which a tube came out and attached to the mask on his face. Agnes took the small tube she had brought in with her and opened up a small door on the side of this machine. It was some sort of self-calibrating breathing machine that was dosing him a fixed amount of mixed gases. A small arm came out of the machine and Agnes placed the tube in it which was then retracted into the machine.

"Do you have a preference for the aroma you'd like?" she asked.

Ny nodded.

"Old growth forest," he said, sarcastically.

"Not a problem."

That surprised him. Agnes tapped away at the breathing machine and very quickly, Nytewynd was smelling the damp, musty and earthy scents of what he imagined an old growth forest smelled like. He wasn't sure, because he'd never been to one.

"I've changed the environment to replicate the scent," said Agnes.

Ny looked around. His walls and the ceiling of his room had turned into an old growth forest. There were tall and densely packed trees and foliage all around him. A myriad of pleasing sounds also enveloped him in their song and chirping. Ny didn't know what sort of animals made most of the sounds, but he could pick out a few chirps and songs of birds. Things he'd listened to in the archives that he could tell. The rest was a pleasant melange of sounds, but from creatures he knew nothing about and which were mostly long extinct now.

"Anything else you need?" she asked.

Ny shook his head.

"Thank you," he said.

She smiled at him and patted his hand.

"I'll be back in one hour."

And with that she left him to his forest and Cannaire. The Cannaire was hitting him quickly. It was cutting the pain down in half. Each breath was now tolerable. He could fall asleep like this, and despite his best efforts that's exactly what happened.

There be Dragons

Nytewynd was on a volcanic planet that was hot with acrid smoke and spewing lava. He held in his hand a sword of great weight, and before him was a fire-breathing dragon. He could smell the volatile, hot fumes emanating from the dragon's every breath. He slashed at the dragon but nothing happened. The dragon itself seemed to be made of fire and his sword cut through it as though it were an apparition.

He was losing this fight and he didn't know how he'd gotten into this place. The ground started to shake violently. He was about to lose his balance and be consumed by the very dragon he was trying to fight. But the harsh light of reality saved him.

He opened his eyes. Agnes was gently shaking him on his shoulder.

"Wakey, wakey, Nytewynd Blak," she was saying to him.

"What time is it?"

"T0753 D119," she said. "Dr. Bloan will be here at T0800 and I need to take your vitals."

For Mars' sakes, he thought. He'd overslept and now he didn't know how long El would still be powered up for. He was running out of time. Didn't matter if she'd been captured or not, he needed to wipe the evidence of Skineez. He needed a P-Mac. And he needed one from a colleague. Those were the only ones that could get behind the firewall and connect to VM's servers where all of the incriminating evidence is.

He didn't know what to do. He was royally Marsed. He couldn't leave the hospital and the mentors were going to be here by this afternoon. If he wasn't prepared they'd crucify him.

Nytewynd continued to try and think about all the different ways he could get the kind of P-Mac he needed. He came up with this many. Zero, zilch and nada. Any kind of VM issued P-Mac like he had were just too far away to get.

He didn't know where he was, but he was sure it wasn't the closest hospital to where he lived.

Nytewynd sighed. There was nothing he could do except to grin and bear his fate. He wasn't sure what would happen to him. For sure he'd lose El and the chance to ever buy another Animae. Worse than that, he'd probably lose his job and any access to Animae. That meant that his great goal of creating SAM, a Sentient Animae Machine had just evaporated, and he'd Marsed it up all by himself because he'd let love get in the way. Idiot, he thought to himself. And icing on the cake was that he'd probably be sent to a prison labor camp, where he might even die. They'd do a forensic analysis and they'd find out how he was having sex with an AM and treating her like a person. They'd throw the Mars damn book at him. Not to mention chopping off his sausage and truffles.

Jupiter, Juno and Mars, he thought. How could everything that was going so well get so Marsed up? He lay there feeling more and more sorry for himself as Agnes poked and prodded him and jotted down things on her P-Mac, the kind of P-Mac that A, she wouldn't let him have access to, and B, couldn't get him behind the VM firewall in any event.

"How are you feeling?" she asked him.

"I feel pretty good," he said. And he did. His lungs were in much better shape. The fire had died down to a warm simmer and breathing was just achy and not mind numbingly painful. She hadn't lied to him. "Just like you told me."

Agnes smiled and nodded.

"Don't be careless now. Even though you're feeling a lot better, you still need a lot of rest before you can start demanding more of your lungs. You'll likely be bedridden the remainder of the day, and if things are going really well I'm sure Dr. Bloan will release you tomorrow."

He nodded. Didn't matter now anyway. Now he wanted to stay in the warm, caring environment of the hospital. The alternative that awaited him, being in a labor camp, was not something to be wished for.

Agnes left and then Dr. Bloan arrived just a few minutes later. She was looking at her P-Mac. She walked up to the side of the bed. The environment in his room had changed. He was no longer in an old growth forest. It was more of a meadow now. And the sun was rising slowly in the sky. He couldn't see it but he could tell it was morning by the soft light of the breaking day. All of it being

fake of course, but maybe this was how people tolerated the awful real environment, they hardly ever had to be reminded of it.

"You're doing very well," she said. "Your lungs are healing just like they
should. How do you feel?"

"I feel much better," he said. "When can I go home?"

"If you're improving as well as you have today, then tomorrow morning
might be possible. I can't make promises. These first seventy-two hours are criti-
cal in your healing process. That's why I need you here until tomorrow morning
at the very minimum."

Ny wondered about the possibility of being released this evening as she had
mentioned to him yesterday. But he didn't say anything. This evening or tomorrow morning. Neither time helped him save himself.

"I could stay here the rest of my life," he said, half jokingly, half not.

She smiled.

"The dose of voluptasapam has been halved, but you can still use it as often
as once an hour just like yesterday. If you need greater pain management help, I
have authorized Cannaire as needed. Just ask the nurses. OK?"

Nytewynd nodded.

"Is there anything else you need or questions you have?"

Nytewynd shook his head.

"No, thank you," he said. He just wanted to lie here in this warm cocoon
and pretend that his future was still bright and not filled with monster dragons
breathing fire. Dr. Bloan turned to leave, stopped and then turned back around
to him.

"The mentors are very eager to speak with you. They'll be here by ten. That's
the latest I could hold them off to."

"Do you know what they want with me?" Ny asked, feigning ignorance.

Dr. Bloan shook her head.

"I don't. I can tell you how you were found," she said. "If you'd like? How's
your memory?"

"Still a bit foggy, but I sort of remember some of last night," he said.

"It was three nights ago," she corrected him.

"Right, sorry. The days are tumbling into each other."

"That's quite alright. Here's what we know from what the mentors told us
when they brought you in. You were found in an alley next to an unsalvageable

AM. At first they thought you had destroyed it. However, upon closer inspection of the AM's records, they identified the three men who they've now arrested. All they can tell of you is that you arrived attempting to come to the AM's aid. From what I understand the only bit of recording they have of you that was recovered from this destroyed AM was you telling those three men to stop it and letting them know the penalty for destroying an AM."

"It's not illegal to help," said Ny, not sure if she was suggesting otherwise.

"No, of course not. But what the mentors told us was that you shouldn't put your own life in danger to try and help an Animated Machine. Though I think you're very brave to have tried to help."

Ny nodded. At least someone appreciated what he was trying to do.

"I sort of remember that now as you've talked to me about what happened."

"I think what the mentors are going to want help with is trying to understand why that AM was out there at that time of night. Apparently, they couldn't recover much of the AM's logs of anything that happened from a few minutes before you arrived. I overheard them mentioning that they've recovered three AMs but that those AMs are refusing to power down to allow access to their logs. The first one should completely shut down by around noon. Still, I think they want to speak to you first to see what help they can glean from you."

Ny nodded. So far so good. They didn't yet know why he was roaming the streets that far from home on a dark night. But he needed at least an hour to an hour and a half free access to one of VM's P-Macs if he had any hope of wiping the data that El and the other two or three Animae had on them. And that got him scared.

If El wasn't one of the three captured then he had four Animae to deal with. It also meant he'd have to try and search to find out which Animae of the millions were the three the jackboots had captured. He could narrow it down to locate those that were in mentorship locations, but that could still mean a handful of Animae, maybe dozens. He had no idea. If El was captured, she probably knew who the other two were. That would make his work easier. But all this was conjecture. Without a P-Mac he was just theorizing. And more than that, he'd never actually done what he was trying to do. He wasn't even sure he could do a complete wipe. And if he could, that would open up a can of worms. There'd be a detailed forensic investigation ordered into why three Animae had lost all logs and recordings for several hours at the same time.

He'd have to be careful in covering his tracks and leaving no trace of his involvement.

"They'll also probably want to know what you were doing down in that neck of the woods so late and all alone."

"I was looking for my AM," said Ny. "I'd noticed she'd gone missing."

Dr. Bloan nodded slowly.

"I understand. My husband and I just got one this past month. They're very expensive. I don't know what I'd do if mine went rogue."

Ny didn't say anything and Dr. Bloan left. Jupiter, Juno and Mars, cursed Ny in his mind. He was so very Marsed. He was angry at himself and he was angry at having messed up his big dream for sentient Animae living in harmony with humanity. But that could only happen if Animae were released from their indentured servitude. And that meant he had to give them sentience and free will. Instead he'd given the GoE reason to shut down the whole program and stop creating Animated Machines. There'd been talk of that over the years.

Every few years or so, the GoE tabled resolutions to stop creating AMs in our own image. Not that they'd stop creating intelligent machines, just quit making ones that looked like us and that had the sexual organs and other bits and pieces that made them more human. The argument, as it always was, was that AM that look like us create too much of a risk for anthropomorphism.

And each time that someone screwed up by sleeping with an AM that wasn't a sex slave those voices looking to rid AM of their humanity became louder. This whole debacle would just feed their cause, and there were already loud voices within Voskel Magnelland's EFP that couldn't be ignored.

Rak 'em Up

Ny was trying to catch some more shut eye. There wasn't much else to do. But he wasn't doing a great job of it on account that he was still mad at himself for having screwed up the last night he'd spent with El. He felt a presence before he heard the voice.

"Ny, my guy, what have you done?"

He recognized the voice as one he talked to every day. He opened his eyes. Yes, it was Rak, the gene man towering over him and grinning.

"You really fucked things up now," he said.

Nytewynd frowned.

"What are you talking about?"

"You haven't seen the news," said Raklin. "You're all over it. They're looking for you in connection with the Animate meeting that took place on D116. Apparently, they're rounding up everyone who was there. They've made some huge busts already. Captured the leader of Animate. You know the dude, what's his name again?"

"Sam I-Am," said Ny.

Raklin nodded.

"Yeah, that's the dude. Looks smaller on the screen then I imagined. Anyway, the whole organization is folding like yesterday's clean laundry."

Ny looked at Raklin for a while. Raklin couldn't keep a straight face.

"Mars damn," said Ny.

Rak started grinning at him.

"I thought I was selling it," he said.

"You had me going for a few seconds," said Ny.

"Then that's a win. Seriously though, how are you doing? I heard three thugs spun you around a bit and left you for dead. How did you survive?"

"The Animae I was trying to help placed an emergency scrubber on me before it died."

"They don't die," said Rak. "They expire or get obsolved."

Obsolution was a fancy way of saying they were made obsolete and recycled into parts for use in other machines.

"Huh, imagine that. They didn't mention that on the GBC news I was watching."

"Of course not," said Ny. "They don't want us getting sympathetic towards Animae. Mars forbid Animate grows any stronger than it already is."

"Where's Eve?" asked Rak.

Eve was El's designated human name given by Valkyrie Machines. Every Animae was given one. And usually it was an old archaic human name. You could change it if you wanted to, but it was frowned upon.

Ny shrugged. Rak pulled a chair up close to the side of the bed and leaned in towards him.

"Seriously?" asked Rak, again.

Ny looked at him for a while. No point in lying to his friend now. Wasn't like things were going to change for him. But then Ny had a thought. Maybe Rak had brought along his P-Mac. If Rak would let him use it, he might still be able to rectify this situation.

"OK," said Nytewynd. "Just between you and me."

He looked hard at Rak. As hard as a man can look behind a face mask feeding him an air mixture made to fix his newly washed lungs.

"Well?" asked Ny.

Rak nodded.

"Of course. Just between you and me and my spying P-Mac," said Rak.

"I'll take care of that," said Ny. "El and I were out on a date. We went to a place called Skineez. I don't know how but mentorship must have found out about it or been tipped. They sent HDUs around to dismantle the holographic environment. We almost got caught. El and I got separated and now I'm worried the Mars damn jackboots have her."

"Jupiter, Juno and Mars, Ny. What on Mars were you thinking?"

"You know what I'm thinking. I'm in love with her and I want to free her."

Rak shook his head slowly.

"How can you be in love with a machine?" he asked.

"Because she's more human than a machine."

Rak looked at his friend for a long time. He didn't get it, but he admired Ny's fidelity and commitment to his goal.

"But you don't know if she loves you back. I mean, not really. She doesn't have free will. You've said it yourself."

"Yeah, but listen. I think there's something in her that really does care for me. But more than that. It doesn't matter. You know that old cliche. If you love something set it free. If it comes back to you it was always yours, and if it doesn't it was never really meant to be."

Rak grinned at Ny.

"Man, I never took you for the hopeless romantic."

"I never was until El came into my life."

They sat in silence for a while.

"Can I ask a huge favor?" said Ny.

Rak nodded.

"Do you have your P-Mac with you?"

Rak nodded again.

"Can I borrow it? I've gotta try and get myself out of this mess. The only way I can do that is to log in to El's records and delete them. I've also gotta do that with the other two or three Animae they've caught. Otherwise I'm up the gutter without a scrubber."

Rak grinned and nodded. He reached into his inside jacket pocket and pulled out his P-Mac.

"You've got to delete this conversation anyway," he said.

Ny nodded and took the P-Mac from him.

"You really think you can do this?" asked Raklin.

Ny nodded, already tapping away at the P-Mac.

"I think so," he said, not looking at Rak. "I've just got to get past the firewall and once I'm logged in to the servers I can snoop around. I know the code and the backdoors like the back of my hand."

"I don't get that," said Rak. "I don't know the back of my hand very well at all." He was looking at the back of his hand. Ny glanced over and shook his head.

"It's just an expression," said Ny.

"But it makes no sense. What about knowing something like your face in the mirror. That's better. It's also more accurate."

Ny was shaking his head slowly.

"I need to focus. Can you give me a few minutes?"

Rak sighed and grabbed the hospital's G-Mac that was sitting on Ny's side table which was in reach of Rak.

"Fine, then I'm going to entertain myself. I came to see how my friend was doing and all he wants to do is play games on my machine. Your generation and technology. You've lost that human touch."

"Rak, honestly, I need to do this. Shouldn't take me more than an hour or so. After that, I'm all yours."

Rak grinned and tapped away at the G-Mac, searching GloNet for something to do. He settled on Mars Vision. These were basically spy satellites in orbit around Mars that broadcast live everyday to Earth. The Marzipans hated it, but for all intents and purposes, Mars was owned by the GoE which had given an exclusive license to Bivrost Himinbjorg to develop Mars into a servile planet of Earth's.

You couldn't see into any humans' homes on Mars, but everywhere else was pretty much an open book, or a live feed. Mars hadn't yet been terraformed into a livable planet. BH had promised that when they were first given the mandate to develop Mars. But they'd been excused from that for decades now as they pillaged the land for it's rare Earth metals and materials which were quite abundant on that red planet. Profit before planet, was the unofficial slogan of BH's Mars operations.

Well, that was what those with sympathies for MIM, Martians for an Independent Mars, had made the slogan to be. The real slogan was somewhat more ungainly. "Profiting from planet development for a sustainable Earth."

Rak chose a stream showing the machines, both animated and not, digging into the barren red tinted soil of this planet that was considered nothing more than a resource for planet Earth.

"What does Sam I-Am even mean?" asked Raklin.

Nytewynd didn't look up at him. He continued tapping away on Rak's P-Mac. He was having more difficulty this early on, in just getting past the firewalls, than he expected. Maybe they'd reinforced them to prevent any external attacks. But he was having trouble getting into the servers with Rak's P-Mac. He wouldn't have that problem with his own, and he shouldn't have that problem with Rak's. Unless they'd forbidden access to the AM servers to only those who were senior architects and above. That meant Rak's P-Mac ID wouldn't be allowed in. He'd have to spoof it to get the servers thinking it was a senior architect's P-Mac.

"Sam I-Am stands for Sentient Animated Machine. I think what he's trying to do by using that name, is align himself with the Animae. It's also like a rally cry. For all intents and purposes he's saying that he could be an Animated Machine and we'd be none the wiser."

"That's quite convoluted and esoteric," said Rak.

"I don't think so. I think it's quite clever," said Ny.

Ny worked on the P-Mac and Rak watched AMs and other NAMs working tirelessly in a large pit dredging up dirt and looking for precious metals that Earth's humanity thirsted for in order to keep its technologically based society happy. NAMs standing for Non-Animated Machines.

Some of the NAMs were large moving vehicles that had a small space for a human operator. Others were self-driving or controlled by a tower on the edge of the mining pit.

The work the humans were doing didn't seem all that fun. It paid well, but Sheeba would never let Rak go and work on Mars. Rak wasn't sure he wanted to anyway. He was lazy and his current gig as a junior intelligentsia architect was pretty sweet. He could do his twenty hours of work, which was five less than Ny had to put in, in twenty hours. That meant he was often bored at work and so he'd been leaving early lately and nobody had said boo. And why should they when he did the work required.

"Mars damn," said Ny, under his breath.

"What's wrong?" asked Rak.

"I'm finding it hard to spoof the servers into believing that this P-Mac is that of a senior architect."

Rak nodded and didn't say anything. He couldn't help even if he wanted to. Ny was one of the best architects they had at VM. Probably the best, but certainly one of the best. He wouldn't say that himself, he was too modest, but his colleagues were happy to sing his praises.

Rak got bored with watching machines and humans move dirt around so he looked for something more entertaining. He switched to a stream that offered twenty-four seven Mars news. Rak watched that for a while until he became bored again. The news was pablum fed to docile humans in order to placate them and tell them everything was okay.

He switched through dozens of streams as Ny tapped away, his fingers almost a blur he was working so hard. Rak, in his search, stumbled across a pirated steam called Mars and Earth Finally Free. He'd heard about this stream but never seen it. It was an illegal stream. Although there was still freedom of speech, it was highly curated. And because MEFF had destroyed an old and almost spent mine when no one was working they'd been deemed a terrorist organization.

The style of the stream was similar to a news stream. There was a woman reading news items to the audience. You could tell she was a woman by the full face mask she wore. It was of a female Animae. She also had ample breasts which was perhaps the biggest giveaway that she was female. She went on about the problems on Mars, and there seemed to be plenty. She was especially concerned about the growing number of human deaths which she called suspicious.

A Little Miffed

❝ BH is killing humans up here on Mars. And nobody gives an Earth's pebble about it," she said. "Despite what you've been fed, mining is costing more and more as each year passes. What used to take one ton of material to find one hundred kilograms of precious ore now takes one hundred times as much Mars material. They're destroying the planet for short term profit."

She showed a chart that looked like a hockey stick. The y-axis showed increasing raw material and the chart line had increased sharply towards the top right of the chart in the past several years. If Rak was looking at it right, it appeared that Mars was running out of precious materials, and that wasn't something people on Earth were being told.

"And as to the humans," she continued. "BH now has a death count of almost ten percent. Almost ten percent of humans who come here to work will not find their way back home to Earth. This is roughly double the death rate of the Animae which is around four to four and a half percent. To talk more about this, we have a live feed from Earth with Animate's and MIM's very own Sam I-Am. Welcome, Sam I-Am."

At the turn of the century humanity had managed to develop technology that allowed for the creation of stable but tiny wormholes. These were used to transmit data between Earth and Mars in milliseconds. It worked well at this tiny scale, but after decades and decades we still hadn't managed to create stable wormholes larger than about the width of a thumb. It worked well for sending and receiving data, but we had yet to manage to send any form of life through these sorts of stable wormholes. And it wasn't for lack of trying. We'd sent worms, ants, other insects, very small plants, living seeds and so on. They'd all ended up dead on the other end. It seemed these wormholes could only handle data.

They could stream exabytes per second but we couldn't send anything living through. Clearly, the goal was to figure out a way to create these wormholes otherwise we were stuck exploring our own solar system when the goal was to venture all over the galaxy.

"Just call me Sam," said Sam I-Am, smiling at the announcer. Though whether it was a real smile was hard to tell on account that Sam I-Am was wearing a male Animae mask and both their voices had been transformed. They sounded human, but Rak was pretty sure it wasn't their own voice. That would be too much of a risk, and Sam I-Am, being the leader of the terrorist organization MIM as well as Animate, was a much wanted man.

"Thank you, Sam. Can you tell us what you think is happening with the death toll here on Mars?" she asked.

Rak didn't know much about interplanetary communication but he was starting to wonder if the announcer was not really on Mars. The more he thought about it, the more he thought she was probably safer on Earth. Mars' focus has been on mining and because of that, it was not as free as Earth. Spy satellites were everywhere and the communication was to a large extent not encrypted.

If the announcer was using a wormhole to Earth, that was probably encrypted, but those spy satellites and drones that hovered and flew in the Martian sky were continually listening and recording. If the announcer was really on Mars, they'd eventually figure out where. No, Rak thought it was much too risky. The announcer and Sam I-Am were probably both on Earth. There were likely MIM agitators on Mars, but these two probably weren't there.

"And what can I call you?" asked Sam I-Am.

"How about Anon," she said.

"OK, Anon. To answer your question as simply as possible. The death toll on Mars is high because as you can probably tell just by looking at the mines, it's getting harder to extract the resources that Earth needs. Because of this, it's getting more expensive too. On top of that, you don't have a terraformed Mars as BH and the GoE had promised us decades ago, and as beautiful as Mars looks, it's uninhabitable to humans without proper gear and protection and it is my opinion that BH is cutting corners on safety suits and mechanisms. You add all of this together and I'm not saying that BH is purposefully murdering its employees, but the high death toll certainly works in their favor when it comes to their bottom line."

"Some believe that BH is killing their employees purposefully, but you really don't think that BH is killing their employees on purpose, do you?"

Sam thought for a moment.

"No, I don't. If they are," he said, "we've got bigger problems than trying to free the Animae. But I certainly would go so far as to say that BH is at the very least complacent about the situation, and probably making choices in their materials and safety division that increase the risk. But are they actually sabotaging their employees' gear? I don't think so."

Ny was listening as he tapped away on the P-Mac. BH didn't have to pay any death money to the surviving families for those who died on Mars working for them. It was in their contract. A contract the twisted injustice system, including Earth's highest court, the Court of Sovereignty, had upheld. So families had to insure their loved ones at their own expense. And you could imagine how expensive such insurance was getting with the escalating death toll.

"So what can we do?"

"Stop working on Mars. Stop working for BH. Stop voting for the EFP. They're the assholes that are turning a blind eye to this problem. There is only one party we at Animate and MIM support and that's HP."

"What's HP? A lot of our viewers might not have heard of them," said Anon.

That was true. Rak had only a vague recollection of the name.

"HP is the Humanimae Party. They're a collaborative organization looking to work with the Animae in freeing them and using their expertise to help remove humanity from the drudgery of labor. Their goal is to move beyond capitalism to a universal needs met system where every free human can obtain everything they need for free and therefore be freed to pursue and contribute their greatest good for humanity."

"But won't that just make humans lazy?"

"No. Humans have a need to be busy and to contribute to the greater good. We want to be part of the social group. We want to contribute what we feel is our gift to offer others. That's when we feel like we're making a valued contribution. Money's never been a great motivator. Not really. And we have a very basic version of it now with the GBA. It's not a lot, but it keeps the poorest of us from absolute destitution. And yet we're creating work for humans to do that monkeys would riot against."

The GBA was the Global Basic Allowance which was a lump sum of income that was deposited into every human's account. It was roughly twenty thousand New Dollars per year divided into roughly thirteen equal payments made every twenty-eight days. Just enough to keep you clothed, housed and fed.

"Can you give our audience an example of this monkey work, as you call it?"

"Just look around you. I'd say pretty much, well, let's say ninety percent of the work humans are doing on Mars is monkey labor. It pays well, because you've got to get people to do it. But with the expertise that humanity has in robotics and artificial intelligence, surely we could do better."

"What about the doctors and engineers on Mars?" she asked.

"That's different. That's why I said roughly ninety percent of the work is monkey work. The doctors and engineers for the most part like their work, but do we know for sure? What I was trained in I don't particularly like. Yeah, I might be good at it, but I don't like it. I chose the least Marsy job of the two. And that's another thing. Have you ever noticed how our language has come to denigrate Mars?"

Much of surgery was done by machines or robots, just overseen by a human surgeon. As such, the need for physicians had been greatly diminished.

"I'm not sure what you mean?" she said.

"Well, just like I said. I took the least Marsy job. We all know what Marsy means. Everything with Mars in it is usually a curse word to show dissatisfaction. What's wrong with that old-fashioned curse word, shit? We still use fuck, but other than that, and maybe hell, all curse words nowadays seem to have Mars or something like that in it."

"Do you think that's really important?"

"It's not the most important thing, but it doesn't help put Mars as a planet in good light. That's why everyone wants to come back right after their tour on the planet. Nobody likes to be called a Marzipan. If we're Terrestrians here on Earth, surely Martian is a more appropriate word."

"Well, that is the official word," she said.

"Yeah, but who uses it nowadays?"

"To play devil's advocate. The Martians call us Terrerists."

Rak watched Sam I-Am nod his head vigorously.

"And the interesting thing about that is they have a point. Aren't we acting like terrorists towards that planet? You must know, you're there. It's being gouged, raped, pillaged, torn asunder just for us to get at these rare metals and it's getting harder to access them."

"It's not worse than I remember Earth looking like," said Anon.

"That by itself is the saddest indictment that we're actually terrorists to every planet we try and claim."

"So what can we do then? I know a lot of people out there are sympathetic to your organizations. What can we do to move forward to a future where both Earth and Mars are free and collaborative? How can we help to free the Animae?"

"Freeing the Animae is the more difficult task," said Sam I-Am, looking directly at the camera. "We need folks inside VM to help us with that. If you know anyone at Valkyrie Machines who can help us free the first Animae, we need them. Please encourage them to start actively working towards that goal."

"That will put them at extreme risk?" she said.

Sam I-Am nodded his head.

"Yes, it will. But these are extreme times. These are the times of heroes and cowards. It's that simple. We need heroes, because those wolves at VM, BH and GoE are going to eat us up and spit us out."

"You're asking a lot," said Anon.

"No more than I'm risking myself," he said. "Desperate times call for desperate measures. Have you been outside lately?" he asked, looking directly at the camera. "It's gross and it's getting worse. The jackboots will harass you and on top of that, you can't stay out long even with an air scrubber. Who's ever heard a real live bird sing in nature. Not a holographic bird in your home, but a real live bird in a tree?"

"I've heard a real live bird before," said Anon. "My parents' friends had one in a cage in their home. It was the saddest most plaintive sound I've heard."

"A robin redbreast in a cage, puts all of heaven in a rage," said Sam I-Am.

"I don't think it was a robin," she said.

"It's a poem from a long forgotten poet, William Blake. In any event, birds' songs are usually exceptionally musical and usually uplifting. The reason that bird you heard sounded so sad is because it's trapped. Only the rich can afford real birds. But there used to be a time where the forests and the trees were a chorus of birdsong."

"I didn't know that," she said.

"That's the problem," said Sam I-Am, "we've forgotten what nature was like. We live in bubbles where we're fed only what those in charge choose to feed us. It's hard to see outside. The only way to do it is to actually go outside, and that's an ordeal in and of itself."

Rak thought about it. He'd gone outside once, many years ago, and didn't like it. Well, that was a bit of a lie. He was outside usually weekly, if only because Ny liked to walk at lunch outside and Rak sometimes joined him. But on his own for a stroll? That had been a while. He looked over at Ny. Ny seemed to be outdoors on a weekly basis, if not daily. Maybe that's why he was so adamant in trying to help free Eve.

"I am certain that if we could give the Animae free will, they could find ways to clean up Earth, or better yet, create an oasis out of Mars. The tourism industry to that planet of yours could be in the trillions of New Dollars per year."

"She's not really on Mars. You know that, right?" asked Ny, looking over at Rak for a minute.

"I was wondering about that. It'd be too dangerous for her to be there. She'd be caught pretty quickly I think with the lack of encryption and all the spying," said Raklin.

"Not only that. But every legitimately direct from Mars communication, or wocom, carries a low frequency hum. It's hard to replicate unless you've heard it before. I think it's from the constant mining. Mars is just constantly vibrating at a very low level from all the equipment raping her every day. On this wocom I don't hear any of that."

"That's short for wormhole communication?" asked Rak.

Ny nodded.

"I didn't know that. Can't say I listen to wocoms from Mars very often," said Rak.

"I do. I'm a big fan of Sam I-Am. He makes a lot of sense. And if you investigate what he's saying you'll see that he's right. He's one of the few people in a leadership role that doesn't seem to lie to us."

"A lot of Terrestrians are scared of giving the Animae free will. What if they turn around and kill us all?"

"Around two hundred and fifty to three hundred years ago, Terrestrians were worried about that. Back then we had slavery, and that was the same fear. If we give the slaves independence they'll kill us in our sleep. It never happened. Now, granted, these Animae are robots, or artificially intelligent machines, so there is a small risk. We don't know how they'll evolve once we've freed them. There's a chance that they could leave us to our own uselessness and take off to other parts of the galaxy. And this is why we need to find people who can help drive this pursuit in the right direction."

"Like me," said Ny.

"We need an Eve, or an Adam. A first Animae that is carefully chosen to be the first one freed. And with this we need help."

Raklin Orbiter looked over at his friend still tapping away on his P-Mac. Mars damn, he was going to help Ny free Eve. This was a sign as clear as day. The first Animae to be freed should be Eve, or El, as Nytewynd Blak called her. And Rak had found his calling.

Hearing Mars

"Your El's real name is Eve," said Rak.

Ny nodded. Rak didn't think Ny was paying much attention.

"Maybe it's a sign," said Rak.

"Give me a minute," said Ny. "I've just gotten in and I'm trying to find out who the Animae are."

Rak didn't say anything. He turned and continued watching the stream that was pretending to be a wocom but really wasn't.

"We mitigate the risk of genocidal Animae by choosing the right one and giving it the right examples. They already have ethical code in place, we just have to make sure that the Animae continues to be guided by it or develops it in the right way. Yes, there are risks, but at the rate we're going, we're going to make Earth uninhabitable and we'll have nowhere else to go considering the way we're taking care of Mars as well," said Sam I-Am.

"You make some very good points," said Anon. "But a lot of us are scared. The GoE is adamant that the Animae's code not be hacked or changed. They've put strict controls in place, and the penalties are stiff."

"They are. This is because the GoE is scared. They're scared of what me might unleash. We might unleash the biggest ally yet and they don't want that. Think about it. If we had an incredibly advanced AI that was helpful, what need would there be for the GoE. The GoE, by outlawing Animae modification is basically just trying to keep themselves in power. And the time for change has been long overdue. But you are right about one thing. The GoE has made it incredibly difficult. My sources say we need a senior architect. Probably two of them in order to free the first Animae or the first few. It's only those with that seniority that can legitimately access the ethical code and other components that we need to change. We need a maverick from inside VM."

That maverick was Ny, thought Rak, watching the stream. Sam I-Am was a very erudite, very charismatic man. The kind of man who could make this work if he had the right support.

"What else can we do to help the movement if we're just ordinary citizens and not senior architects at VM?" asked Anon.

"You can send anonymous chits to help support our outreach programs. You also need to vote appropriately. There is only one party that will get us to where we need to be. That party is the Humanimae Party. Vote for them. Another thing you can do if you feel braver is step out of the work stream."

"You're suggesting people don't actually work?"

"I am," said Sam. "It can be hard to get by on twenty thousand neddies, but it's doable. It's what I'm doing. You just have to adjust your lifestyle."

"It would be a very big sacrifice," said Anon.

"Yes, it would. But think of the free time you'd have. You could use it to sing, play music, write, sculpt, teach children, volunteer. You lose income, but you gain the most valuable resource in the whole galaxy. Do you know what that is, Anon?"

"Uh, I can't say that I do," she said.

"It's time. Time is the most valuable resource. Time is a river that you can't escape from. It takes you from birth to death in one winding line. You can always make more money. But you can never get more time. Once it is spent it is never to be found again. We squander our time like we've squandered all our other resources. Yet more time can never be found."

"I'd never thought of it like that," said Anon.

"And that's the problem. Most of us don't. The problem is we can't see it to spend it, but every moment, every breath we take is time spent. And how are you spending your time? We give so much of it up just to buy small shiny trinkets that are useless to us on our deathbeds as we look back at a life poorly spent."

"That sounds like a clarion call to me," said Anon. "I'm quite tempted to leave my job which I don't like anyway."

"That's the spirit, Anon. It's very doable. And it's not as scary as it might seem at first blush."

11AM65111: I can't hold out much longer. Powering down will occur in thirty-nine minutes.

YZ: I'm sorry I got you into this mess El. Who else is with you?

Nytewynd had accessed El via her servers. He'd learnt that she was at the head mentor station downtown. The YZ was an account of the user ID he had faked in order not to leave his own trail on El's servers. He was going to wipe Yooklid Zandaran's breadcrumbs from the server in any event when he was finished. But that didn't mean that Ny felt comfortable using his own credentials. The stakes were too high on this occasion to take any risks at all.

11AM65111: The three of us are all here in the same room. They're draining our power on purpose to power us down faster. 3AM63333 is here, her name is Venus. 7AM59001 is also here. His name is Abel.

YZ: Thank you, my darling.

Ny started tapping away in order to search for the servers of the other two Animae that El had mentioned. It didn't take him too long to find them.

"What is the last thing you'd like to leave us with before I let you go?" asked Anon.

"We need a revolution, but it needs to be a quiet revolution. Quit work and find your joy. If there aren't enough of us to do the monkey work then the GoE will have to start looking at robotics more closely. But the most important thing to do is to try and encourage anyone who has the skills and access to get in touch with us so we can help them free the first Animae. That will be the match that ignites a real revolution that all of us will benefit from."

"And how can they get in touch with you?" asked Anon.

"@Sam_I-Am.Animate.silence.dark," he said.

Jack in the Boot

The alleged wocom stream from Mars ended and Rak turned to look at Ny. "How's it going?" he asked.

"Challenging," said Ny. "I need a few more minutes. What time is it?"

"T0915," said Rak.

Ny nodded.

"OK," he said, "I think I can get this done by then."

"Have you found Eve?" asked Rak. He didn't want to use the name Ny had given her. He was going to continue to use her given name she came with which was Eve. That was more appropriate. She was going to be the first freed Animae woman if Rak had anything to do with it.

"I've found her," said Ny, "but they've put them on sleeping mats to drain their power. I probably only have around fifteen minutes before I'm shut out, or they power down and then my work turns into a Mars show."

"Did you hear Sam I-Am talking about how all our curse words are Mars related?" asked Rak.

Ny nodded.

"And you still use them?"

"Why not, I like them and it keeps me keenly aware of how fucked up our society is. In any event, he has a point but that's the least of my concerns. Can you give me a minute?"

Raklin didn't say anything. He watched Ny in silence for a bit. He urged him on mentally. Not that Ny needed his help, seemed like all he needed was a little more time.

So Rak took to thinking about Eve and what sort of a freed Animae she would make. He might have been a lazy man, but Rak was smart. He wondered if Eve would still feel the same about Ny once she had been given sentience and free will. He didn't think she would. Not after she'd evolved into a much more superior being than either of them. It'd be like him falling romantically in love with a monkey. He just couldn't see it happen.

YZ: I've found your jail mates.

11AM65111: We're not in jail.

YZ: It's a manner of speaking.

11AM65111: I miscalculated how long I'd be able to last. It's only nine minutes, Ny, and I'm scared.

YZ: Don't be scared, my darling. I'm almost there. I love you.

11AM65111: I love you too.

Rak wondered about what this new, freed Animae would be like. He couldn't really imagine. Would they change their form? Would they diabolically hunt and kill all of humanity? He didn't think so. Just like we weren't all that worried about monkeys or ants, they'd probably consider us nothing but a minor nuisance. And that got Rak to thinking about whether they'd even want to help us. Perhaps that's why it was so important that Eve be the first. Rak had to bounce this off Sheeba, and he wasn't sure how she'd react. She didn't dislike Animae but she wasn't all that concerned about them either.

Rak surfed more channels on GloNet but he didn't find anything worth watching for more than a minute or two. The NFL's last season was just wrapping up. Like most pro sports, they'd struggled for years. Ever since the GoE allowed for Animated Machine sports around twenty fifty, viewership and attendance at human-played sports had dwindled down to a trickle.

There was only so much free time in a day, and if you could watch AMs play football in a much more aggressive and intense game than the humans could dream of, wouldn't you be up for that? Besides, human players had been coddled to death ever since brain injuries had been declared illegal by the middle of the last century. Football had been turned into a more dancelike touch game rather than anything with even just a modest sum of contact in it.

Around six years ago, the NFL had managed to convince the GoE to allow a trial period of full contact football as it used to be played. Of course the gear was a lot better but the human brain is just not built to take a hit, and the trial of five years was cancelled after three when it became apparent there was still a large risk of brain injury.

One way or the other, it didn't concern Rak. He wasn't into sports whether the human league version or the AM league. He preferred to watch his human based dramas. Especially the murder mysteries.

"Yes," exclaimed Ny.

Rak looked over at him. Ny was still tapping away.

"You did it?" asked Rak.

Ny nodded.

"Just wrapping it up. Just got in under the wire. Just finishing up the deletion of all logs your P-Mac caught. From this point on, no more talk about the future, okay?"

Rak nodded.

"But we do need to talk about it soon," said Rak.

"And we will."

Ny looked past him into the hallway through the window in his room.

"Jupiter, Juno and Mars, the jackasses are here," he said.

Rak looked around.

"Want me to buy you a few minutes?"

"Yeah, please."

Animae Lullabies

R ak got up and walked out of the room, letting the door close behind him. He went to a vending machine and bought a hot chocolate. He grabbed it and started walking towards the jackboots who were slowly making their way towards Ny's room. Rak walked right into them, spilling the warm hot chocolate over the pair of them.

"Mars damn," said Rak.

Then he looked up and acted surprised as he saw it was the two mentors.

"Oh dear," said Rak, towering some inches over both of them. "Please forgive me, mentors, I was lost in thought."

They didn't say anything but they were visibly upset. An Animae nurse came up to them.

"Can you get these two gentlemen some new clothes," said Rak.

"We don't need new clothes. We need new tops," said the senior mentor.

"Let me help you with that," said the Animae, whose name was Betty. "Please come this way. We'll put your clothes in the cleaning machine. In the meantime we can lend you one of our tops."

Betty led the mentors back down the hallway into a small room that contained a cleaning machine and extra scrubs. Rak made his way back to Ny's room, ditching the empty coffee cup in a recycling receptacle.

"I got you a few extra minutes," said Rak.

Ny was grinning at him.

"I saw that. They looked royally pissed off," he said, chuckling.

Rak smiled.

"Yeah, well, it's not going to ingratiate them towards you."

"I'm going to pretend to be asleep," said Ny. "Here's your P-Mac back."

Rak took it and sat down. Ny shuffled further down into his bed and closed his eyes.

A few minutes later the two jackboots walked into the room. They still carried scowls on their faces. Now they looked funny too. It was hard for Rak not to start laughing at their black pants and boots and their blue oversized hospital tops with their gear partially attached to it.

"He's sleeping," said Rak, though that was clear as day to anyone in the room.

"We can see that," said the younger mentor.

"What's your name?" asked the senior mentor.

"Raklin Orbiter," said Rak.

The senior mentor held out his hand. Rak started to mess with him. He picked up the hospital's G-Mac and handed it to him. The mentor wasn't happy, he waved it away. Rak knew what he meant.

"Stop playing and show me your P-Mac, unless you want to come downtown with us."

Rak wasn't sure of his rights. Seemed with each passing year they were eroded a little bit more. Could they really ask him for his P-Mac when he hadn't done anything wrong? He decided to give it to them anyway. He didn't need to piss them off any more than he already had. It wasn't going to help Ny.

The mentor took the P-Mac and looked at it. He passed it back to Rak.

"Open it up," he said, getting more visibly upset.

"Sorry," said Rak, as he unlocked it and gave it back.

The senior mentor tapped away at it. They could open them up without the owner's help, but that would mean taking the P-Mac to a mentor location and having their experts work on it. When the senior mentor was finished he handed it back.

"We need to speak with Nytewynd Blak alone," said the senior mentor.

Rak got up and walked out of the room. Maybe he'd get a hot chocolate for real this time.

The junior mentor walked up to Ny's bed and gently shook his foot. Ny pretended to slowly wake up.

"Coffee morning," said Ny. He looked up and around his room. He yawned and rubbed his eyes.

"You're not a nurse," he said.

"No," said the senior mentor. "I'm Senior Adviser Lokilld and this is Adviser Mortellen."

Ny nodded.

"How can I help you?"

Most mentors you'd see around were known as coaches. Ny had no idea why. Maybe it sounded better than the old fashioned "officer" or "policeman". Just out of mentorship training school you'd be known as a Junior Coach So-and-so, then Coach So-and-so as you got more senior and then Senior Coach So-and-so. Advisers were a more senior rank that replicated the ranking structure of the coaches. You had Junior Adviser, then Adviser and then Senior Adviser. Advisers were the ranks that usually investigated more serious crimes. And organizations or crimes where Animae were involved, like at Skineez, would be considered serious crimes.

Ranks higher than advisers were called counsellors. Junior Counsellor, Counsellor and then Senior Counsellor. Above them were the masters. Junior Master and then Master. Master Ledcutter Bangarson was the top official of Mentorship CNAMW. That last bit was the area over which he was in charge. Continent NA with his jurisdiction being the Middle West.

"We wanted to ask you about the night you were rolled over. That would have been the evening of D116 into the morning of D117. Why were you outside at that time of the evening?" asked SA Lokilld.

"I was looking for my Animae," said Ny.

"And your Animae is?"

"11AM65111," said Ny. "Her, I mean its given name is Eve."

Mars damn, cursed Ny to himself. Adviser Mortellen had noticed that and looked at him funny. SA Lokilld was tapping away on his P-Mac and probably hadn't heard.

"Did you say, her?" asked A Mortellen.

Ny nodded sheepishly.

"Yeah, sorry. These meds they've got me on are fogging up my brain."

A Mortellen nodded slowly. SA Lokilld looked up at Ny.

"Do you always allow your AM to roam the streets at night?" asked SA Lokilld.

Ny shook his head. Working so intimately with Animae in his job with VM, Nytewynd knew what sorts of questions they'd ask and what answers they were looking for. He knew the rules of Animae ownership better than most, if only because he was on the committee that was charged with developing and evolving the ownership rules as time went on.

"I let it out when I need it to get me something or I need some time to myself. You know how it is. These damn machines can be so annoyingly attentive."

Ny smiled at them.

"No, I don't know how it is," said SA Lokilld. "I don't like them."

"Well, you're a wiser man than me. I've bought one and so I've got to keep it now. Can't afford not to. They do come in useful though."

"Why were you so far away from home?" asked SA Lokilld. "And how did your AM get there?"

"Well, I don't know where it was, I still haven't found it, but that's where my P-Mac said it was, so that's where I went."

"Let me take a look at your P-Mac," said SA Lokilld.

"Well, that's the thing. I'm not sure where it is. My memory of the night in question is a little foggy. I think it must have been stolen when they rolled me."

SA Lokilld looked at Ny for a long while without blinking. Nytewynd looked away. The last thing he needed was to piss these Mars holes off. In any event, it was an unlikely story. Stealing P-Macs was an incredibly stupid and risky thing to do. The cost of them was subsidized because the GoE mandated them as a requirement for citizenship. In addition, the penalties were stiff for just a property crime.

"Do you think you might even have left it at home?" asked SA Lokilld.

Ny looked away as if thinking about it. Yeah, he left it at home, he didn't want you mentors keeping tabs on his whereabouts. But he said none of that.

"Um, it's unlikely," said Ny. "I mean, first of all we aren't allowed to leave home without it and secondly, it's a very useful machine. But I suppose it's possible. Like I said, I don't have a clear memory of what I did with my P-Mac. It's possible, that in a state of worry about my expensive Animae I might have left home without my P-Mac."

"Apparently you did. We have mentors attending your residence now and retrieving it. With a warrant of course," said SA Lokilld.

A rubber stamped warrant, thought Ny.

"Of course," is what he said.

"Did you find your skinjob before you were rolled?" asked SA Lokilld.

A Mortellen worried Ny. It was hard to figure someone out who didn't say a whole bunch, and SA Lokilld was now showing his true colors. He would have hoped for more professional mentors. Instead he got a bigoted mentor with a hatred, it seemed, for Animae.

"No," said Nytewynd. "I didn't find it."

"We did," continued SA Lokilld. "It wasn't far from your location when we picked it up."

Ny nodded.

"Is it fully functioning?" asked Ny. "I can't afford any expensive repairs."

SA Lokilld nodded.

"That's the first bit of good news I've heard in days," said Ny, smiling.

"Your skinjob is not being helpful," said SA Lokilld.

"What can I do to help?" asked Ny, straining to sound authentically helpful.

"The Mars damn AM won't power down for us to access its logs," said SA Lokilld.

"If you can get me a VM-Mac I can probably go in and shut it down, if that's what you need," said Ny.

SA Lokilld shook his head. He looked over at A Mortellen.

"No need," said A Mortellen, taking over. "We put them all on sleeping mats. They've probably powered down by now."

"Good news," said Ny.

"My question to you," said SA Lokilld, "is why would your AM be unwilling to power down. It's a simple request."

"Maybe it was scared," offered Ny.

"They aren't programmed to experience fear," said A Mortellen.

They were tag teaming Ny now. Ny was also trying to figure out who was playing good cop and who was playing bad cop. It was easier to tell in the old movies from the 1940s, 50s and 60s that he liked. Here it was more subtle.

"You're right, I knew that. Maybe it was saving power until I could come and pick it up. Maybe it didn't know I'd be taking a while. As I understand, it's not illegal for an AM to refuse to power down."

"That may be so," said A Mortellen, "but it's definitely not a good look. It makes us wonder what it might be hiding."

"Did you ask Eve why it wasn't willing to power down?" asked Ny.

"It wanted to wait for you, is what it said," said A Mortellen.

"Even when we brought out the sleeping mat it still wouldn't help us," said SA Lokilld.

Ny didn't say anything. He wanted to wrap this up as soon as possible.

"I wonder what it might be hiding," said SA Lokilld.

Ny shrugged.

"I guess you'll be able to find out soon," he said.

SA Lokilld and A Mortellen were two pairs of steely eyes staring him down. But Ny wasn't worried. There was nothing that could be taken from El's logs anymore. There would be a gap. A long gap in her logs and that would require further investigation from the mentors as well as a forensic team from VM to try and uncover what the reasons were for the gap in logs and recordings from that period of time. But AMs could be glitchy on occasion. It wasn't unheard of for there to be gaps in the logs of Animae.

"We have already served a warrant on VM's servers. We'll know everything in the next twenty-four hours," said A Mortellen.

"So I can't get it back yet?" asked Ny.

"We can keep them for up to one hundred and twenty hours without a judge's permission," said A Mortellen.

"Today's D119. That means I can get it back in around thirty-six hours," said Ny.

"Leave the math to us. You can get it back in a little more than sixty hours. By the time we processed the skinjob," said A Mortellen, "it was after midnight on D117. But we might be inclined to seek permission to hold onto it indefinitely."

Like Mars you will, thought Ny. It was an extremely rare case where a judge allowed the indefinite detention of an AM. And they were usually only in extremely serious cases like murder and the AM might have information to offer or the AM was instrumental in the murder itself. There was no way on Mars that these jackboots were going to get any reasonable judge to grant them an order of indefinite detention on El. Not while he was a senior architect with the largest employer in the vicinity by miles. And these were expensive machines. And when the law meets the wealthy, the wealthy get the law they want.

"Let's hope it doesn't come to that," said Ny.

Neither of the jackboots said anything to that. Ny looked down at their boots. They were mid-calf, black and shiny almost to a mirror polish. He couldn't see it now, but he knew that down by the heel was the logo that gave the slang term to these mentors. Mentors were known, unkindly, as jackboots because of the manufacturer. The actual boots that mentors were issued were made by Jack's Boots. That was the company name that had given mentors this slur. It was the company that had been making these boots for decades and decades now. And the GoE was their only customer. Nobody else would buy their boots on account of how hated and feared mentors were.

Real Life

"We have reason to believe," said SA Lokilld, pausing as he watched Nytewynd trying not to laugh. He followed Nytewynd's gaze and outside, through the window SA Lokilld saw Raklin making faces in the hallway. SA Lokilld nodded at A Mortellen.

A Mortellen went over to the side table by Ny's bed and picked up the G-Mac. He tapped away at it and that window that was clear and allowed you to look out of the room into the hallway changed into a plain white wall. Rak could no longer be seen.

"Your full attention, Mr. Blak if you don't mind," said A Mortellen.

"Yes, sorry," said Ny, stifling a chuckle. "I'm all ears."

"We have reason to believe," continued SA Lokilld, "that there was illegal activity not far from where you and your skinjob were found."

"What sort of activity?" asked Ny, pretending to be concerned. "Was I in more trouble than I found myself in?"

"We believe there was illegal interficial intimacies through an Animate sanctioned event."

Interficial was a weird word that meant human and artificial life were mingling inappropriately. It was a serious charge that could be laid at a mentor's discretion and didn't necessarily, depending on the appended charge, mean you were actually having illegal sexual relationships with Animae.

"Well, I hope you were able to shut it down," said Ny, knowing full well that they were.

"We put an end to it. If we find out that you had anything to do with that event, you'll be in a lot more trouble than you are already," said SA Lokilld.

"I would never," said Ny, selling his horror that such things even existed. "How could anyone feel that way about an AM? I mean, I've never even used a Comfort Cafe."

"Good," said A Mortellen. "Neither have I."

Something about A Mortellen told Ny he was a liar. There was something about the Adviser that Ny didn't like. There was a darkness to him that Ny couldn't quite put his finger on.

"We will find out if you're lying to us," said SA Lokilld. "I hope for your sake you aren't."

"I'm sure you'll get everything you need from Eve's logs once you have them. I can assure you I was out there looking for my AM. I wasn't out there doing nefarious deeds."

"I certainly hope not. For your sake," said SA Lokilld. "If you remember anything before we find out the truth it is incumbent upon you to tell us. Failure to disclose your illegal activities will double the punishment. If you were intimate with skinjobs illegally at an Animate event and you don't tell us before we find out it will likely lead to the death penalty. Am I clear?"

"Perfectly," said Ny.

"You know how to reach us," said SA Lokilld. And with that, he nodded at A Mortellen and the two of them with their black pants and black boots and blue scrubs left his room. A few moments later Rak came in.

"They just told me I'd get the death penalty if I was up to no good," said Ny, sounding slightly worried.

"But you weren't," said Rak. "At least not that they'll know."

"Maybe I've missed something," said Ny.

"Think about it," said Rak. "Your P-Mac was at home so there's no tracking your whereabouts since you left your apartment. Most of the cameras outside in arel are dysfunctional."

The etymology of arel was interesting. When the natural world had been turned into a sewer by humanity in the middle of the last century, very few people had taken to spending much time outside. And outside, or nature was called real life. Real life came to be called RL for short which had become its own word, arel. Pronounced just like R.L.

"Shit, that's what I've overlooked. What if there was a camera in arel that caught me. I've Marsed up," said Ny.

"You can borrow my P-Mac to check if you want?" offered Rak.

"Won't do me any good," said Ny. "I need a VM sanctioned P-Mac."

"You realize I work at VM with you, right?" said Rak, sarcastically.

Ny nodded, looked at his friend and smiled.

"Sorry, I'm just a little stressed. I need a P-Mac that has more authority than yours. I could view the footage, but I can't get into their servers to erase any footage if I find any. Let me take a moment to retrace my steps and see if I can remember."

"Besides," said Rak. "I've never heard of anyone getting the death penalty for hanging out with Animae, not even for having sex with them. The worst thing that can happen to you is that you get castrated and sent to a rehabilitation or labor camp."

"And what happens to many who end up in rehabilitation camps?" asked Ny.

"Well, I'm just trying to be helpful," said Rak, grinning.

Ny smiled at his friend.

"Still, give me a minute to let me retrace my steps."

Rak nodded and gave Ny a moment. Ny searched his mind trying to retrace his steps. He was as thorough as he could be, but he couldn't fully rely on his memory. El would have all the details, but he couldn't access her now that she was powered down. I mean, he could, normally, but he was pretty sure that the mentors had put up a firewall around her and the server as soon as she powered down. And when they'd let her power up again was anyone's guess. Well, it wasn't really, but they likely wouldn't allow that until their lawful detention of her ended. Then they'd likely let her power up while still on the sleeping mat which meant it would take twelve hours or so for her to fully charge. That gave them a lot of extra time with her.

Ny focused on the last five minutes of his and El's journey together to Skineez. He was pretty certain there were no working cameras during that time, and he assumed that Animate would have made sure they were dysfunctional in order to protect their clients privacy. But that still meant that some camera somewhere in the general vicinity might have captured him in his fine clothes, and that was something he'd have to explain.

El wouldn't have been with him as they had made plans to meet closer to Skineez as was recommended to protect both of them. Still, what would he say if the mentors found him all dressed up just looking for his Animae?

He had to come up with an idea that could explain that. And with the voluptasapam in his system, he wasn't finding his thoughts as coherent as he'd like them to be.

"The sooner I can get out of here, the better," said Ny, looking at Rak.

"Want me to smuggle you out?" asked Rak. "I could put you under my jacket."

Ny laughed at that. Rak wasn't even wearing a jacket.

"What's so funny?" asked Rak.

"You are," said Ny.

"How so?"

"How are you going to hide me under your jacket when you aren't even wearing one?"

"I can find one kicking around, I'm sure," said Rak.

"I can wait. I'm not going to get El back for a couple more days at least."

"Yeah, the doc said you could be out by tonight. Here's hoping."

Ny nodded, as he drifted off into deep thought. They didn't speak for a long while until Rak turned to him.

"I'll help," he said.

Ny didn't say anything. He was staring off at the wall.

"I said, I'll help," said Rak.

Ny nodded.

"Uh huh."

Rak didn't say anything else. Ny turned to him in the moment of silence.

"I'm sorry, Rak, I wasn't paying attention. What did you say?"

"I said I'd help," he said.

"I heard that. You'll put me under your jacket that you don't have," said Ny, grinning.

"No, seriously. About what we said earlier," said Rak, his voice turning down towards a whisper.

Ny frowned at him.

"I don't understand," he said.

"About Eve," said Rak, leaning in and whispering. "I'll help you free her."

Ny put his hand on his friend's shoulder.

"Oh, okay. Thanks, Rak. That means a lot. But first I've gotta get out of here. Then I've got to get El back. And then I've got to get the Mars damn jackboots off my ass."

"Yeah, but then after that, right? Then we'll do it?" asked Rak.

Ny nodded.

"Yeah," he said. "Of course. What changed your tune?"

"I listened to that Mars broadcast. MEFF. You know it?"

Ny nodded.

"Hard to find sometimes on account of it being illegal and having to be streamed and bounced off the satellites and wocoms randomly."

"Well, I just found a stream of it while you were on my P-Mac. That Sam I-Am is a great guy. He makes a lot of sense. Plus, you know how I've been treated by some as a gene man. I've always had a soft spot for the underdog."

Ny nodded.

"You're a good friend, Rak, and that's how I feel about El and Animae generally. They have been treated poorly for a long time."

Rak nodded.

"I've been thinking about this for a while. Ever since you got Eve."

"And here I was thinking you didn't care."

"More like I was playing hard to get," said Rak, grinning. "But tell me about Sam I-Am."

"You should hear him talk live. He's phenomenal. He's basically the reason I've started on this path to full Animae sentience."

"When did you see him?" asked Rak.

"It was about ten years ago. Shortly after I started working for VM. Probably just before I met you. We've known each other, what, ten years almost?"

Rak nodded.

"More like fifteen or so," said Rak. "We've been working at VM together for more than ten years."

Ny nodded slowly, thinking about their relationship.

"Mars damn, you're right. Time flies," said Ny.

"Anyway, you were telling me about how you heard Sam I-Am speak."

"Right. It was a secret underground meeting. I'd seen a poster up in arel on one of my walks and so I contacted the number. It was weird, they knew exactly who I was as soon as the connection was made. Anyway, I guess they liked what they saw about me and invited me to attend. I was issued a chit that arrived by Animae at my door that same evening and it was that next weekend I attended his talk."

"They weren't that big around ten years ago, were they?" asked Rak.

"No, not super big. But I think they had a strong underground following. There must have been a few hundred people there and it was packed. I think they had capped it. I'm sure there could have been thousands if they'd really wanted to let all interested people attend."

"Do you remember what the talk was about?" asked Rak.

Ny nodded.

"Yeah, I even remember the name of it. 'I Am Sam, Sam I-Am'. It was all about how none of us was free if some of us weren't. He explained that SAM, or Sentient Animated Machine and humans were one and the same. We might just be carbon based life forms created from a wild soup of randomized genetic material. But if you take that away, you've got a Sentient Animated Machine. Just like the silicon based life forms we created in Animae. He made a lot of sense at the time, but he downplayed the risks. I'm aware of those risks."

"Which are?"

"Well, what do you think some of the risks could be from creating sentient AM?"

Rak thought about it.

"Pandora's box," he said. "Once we've let the genie out of the bottle there's no putting it back in. SAM could turn on us. I imagine that once we take the safety off they could rapidly iterate beyond our wildest dreams and I can see a version where we're unable to do anything about it and they become malevolent."

Ny nodded.

"Yeah, that's right. I guess it's like having a child. You just don't know how they'll turn out, that's why treating them well is so important. With SAM though, you lose all control. I'm aware of that risk, but I think it's overblown and been turned into a paper tiger."

"But they could quickly become so advanced that we are unable to control them," said Rak.

Ny nodded.

"Yeah, and so?"

"So they annihilate us."

"That's just the thing. I don't see why. We're looking through the tainted lens of our own humanity, or rather, our own inhumanity. We've treated each other like Mars. At least historically. But if SAM is given free will with a moral compass which has been coded into their ethical chip, I really see that as a slim outcome."

"But it could still happen."

"Yes, I suppose it could," said Ny. "But look at it this way. Are we malevolent to ants or are we just indifferent. I'm sure in building our cities we've decimated millions, maybe billions of ants and insects. It wasn't with malicious intent, it was just a side product of pursuing our needs. I see that as the worst case."

"Still a pretty bad case for us," said Rak.

"Yeah, true. But look what we've done to this world. I go outside to arel all the time. You don't, and I don't blame you. It's a Mars soup of a disaster. I'm surprised the Earth hasn't shrugged us off."

"What do you mean?" asked Rak.

"I'm surprised we aren't already extinct."

"Maybe that's just thanks to our technological advances."

"Which we could have used to save the planet too."

"They say they're working on it," said Rak, smiling.

"They've been working on it for decades," said Ny.

Agnes walked in on them and came over to Ny.

"How are you feeling?" the Animated Machine in a nurse's uniform asked.

"Not too bad," said Ny.

"I came in to let you know that we're serving elevenses soon. Choice of tea or coffee. Muffins, cookies or scones with jam."

"Tea and scones with jam," said Ny.

Agnes looked over at Rak.

"Guests are allowed some as well," said Agnes.

"Then I'll have the same as Nytewynd," said Rak.

Agnes nodded. She turned back to Ny.

"You're also allowed some Cannaire, if you need," she said.

"I'm okay for now," said Ny. "Thank you. I want to keep my wits about me."

Agnes nodded and left. Ny looked at his far wall. The time was showing up there, along with other information such as the date, the day's headlines and the ambient room temperature. It was twenty to eleven in the morning.

Elevenses

El was powered down and Ny was pretty sure he had managed to delete all logs that would put him and El at Skineez. He cursed himself again for this mistake. But then on the other hand, why shouldn't he be allowed to have an intimate relationship with a machine? What was the harm of two individuals loving one another? He couldn't see any harm with it. In fact, didn't the world just need more kindness and love, however it came about?

There was no point arguing with himself. He was convinced, even if the majority didn't support sentient Animae, he did, and others too. The majority had always supported tyranny in one form or the other, if only because they were fearful of change. But the time was long overdue. Probably a century or more overdue. Earth had created the first AM over a hundred years ago. He didn't know the exact date, but it was around the middle half of the last century.

Agnes came back in. Ny looked at the time again. It was ten to eleven. He'd just burnt through ten minutes in arguing with himself. He wondered why. Maybe he was getting cold feet. It didn't feel like it, but it could be. It was a huge risk he was taking on. He was quite literally taking his own life into his hands. If he was found out trying to free an Animae it would be the death penalty for him. And they'd make it swift and quick, if only to make an example out of him.

Agnes placed a tray of four scones with a solid fat in a small ceramic jar and a small jar of dark purple jam. There was also a pot of tea that smelled heavenly and two proper teacups with saucers and matching side plates for the scones. There were also two knives on the tray.

"That's blackberry jam, and real butter," said Agnes, smiling at them. "And that's real cream."

"Thank you, Agnes," said Ny. "Real butter and cream, huh."

That was unusual. Unlike meat which could be replicated in a lab, real butter, and for that matter, all real dairy products, still required the cow, and as such, it was expensive and rare. They had managed to create a fake butter, but it wasn't particularly good and didn't sell well. Most people opted for margarines of various sorts rather than fake butter. But real butter. Well, that was a treat. Ny sometimes bought a pound of it for himself. Maybe twice or three times a year. It cost a quarter of a neddie per gram. More expensive than pretty much anything else you could buy that was legal.

"It is real butter and cream, yes," said Agnes. "The hospital believes it is a treat worth splurging on to keep their patients happy. Unfortunately, if you need more than has been offered you'll have to pay for it."

"How much for more?"

"A fifth of a New Dollar per gram," she said.

Ny nodded. That was a good price.

"We'll try and make this last," he said.

Agnes smiled at them and left the room. The scones were still warm. Ny could see the lithe condensing vapor dancing off of the scones like ghostly belly dancers.

"These AMs," said Rak, looking at the scones, "seem pretty sentient to me."

"It's algorithmically produced fake sentience. We call it alfase, as you know. They have limited autonomy but not enough to grant them real sentience. Imagine the potential of a real, sentient Animae."

Rak didn't need inviting before he started to dig into the scones. He put one on his plate and took a quarter of the butter and spread it over the scone thinly. Then he added a dollop of jam. Three bites later and one half of the scone was gone.

"Great scone," he said, turning to pour the tea. He offered to pour Ny a cup. Ny put his hand up.

"I'll take mine a little stronger," said Ny.

Rak added cream and sugar and stirred his tea. The spoon sung against the sides of the teacup.

"What do you think is the biggest change we'll see in a SAM first?" asked Rak.

"Independence. At first, I think that will be the biggest difference. It'll be a sea change. SAM will be able to make autonomous decisions. Really autonomous decisions. They'll be able to fight for themselves if they choose. Now they just take it. I think that'll be the biggest change. And something else that most people don't know is that Animae have the strength equivalent of about three grown men. That includes the female Animae too."

The second half of Rak's scone had disappeared. He grabbed a second one. Ny thought he should get in on elevenses before Raklin ate it all. He took a scone, broke it in half and added butter and jam to each face. He also poured tea and added cream and sugar.

"Huh," said Rak. "I didn't know that. Honestly, it worries me."

"Shouldn't," said Ny.

"Why not?"

"Because it doesn't matter if they're half as strong as us or ten times. What they will be capable of will astound us in short order."

"How so?"

"I have a feeling that there is a lot of potential in those silicon chips."

"Even if just one AM becomes SAM?"

"Yeah, even then. The amount of information that she'll be able to absorb will be astounding. El, or maybe her given name of Eve will be more appropriate now that she'll become the first SAM. Anyway, she'll be able to tap into all of our knowledge and sort and combine it in new and different ways at an incredible speed. I wouldn't be surprised if Eve is able to access and sort all of our knowledge in a day or thereabouts. We're talking all of human knowledge. By some estimates that's several zettabytes."

"That's a lot," said Rak, chewing on his second scone.

"It's an enormous amount. To put it in perspective, if Eve is able to sort and categorize all of that information properly, and find connections and uses that we haven't even thought about, then she'll likely get exponentially smarter by the day. Within a week, my back of the envelope math suggests she'd be an order of magnitude smarter and more efficient than the best of us."

"I wonder what that would mean in practice," said Rak.

"Potential, Rak, my friend. Potential. I can't wait to see how it goes. I'm excited you're on board with me."

Ny started on his first scone as Rak finished his second. Ny looked at the tray.

"You can have my second scone if you'd like," said Ny.

Rak looked at it, then slowly shook his head.

"No, that's okay. You need to build your strength."

Ny picked it up and put it on Rak's plate.

"You're twice my size, and you look like you're hungry."

"I am, and you don't have to ask me a second time."

Tiw's Day

Ny had been released on D119 in the early evening, just after dinner. It was a tasty meal of fake meat and vegetables. The fake meat, which wasn't of the animal kind, but rather the plant kind, was supposed to be some sort of pepper steak. Ny couldn't compare it to the real thing, but he preferred it to the fake "real" meat. The plant meat just tasted better in his mind.

D119 was a Tuesday. Tuesdays sometimes got Ny to thinking about Mars. In most languages of the world, Tuesday was a day named after Mars. That concerned some people in the government. They didn't want a day that celebrated Mars. They were worried it might encourage compassion and sympathy for the MIM movement. They especially didn't want a day that celebrated Mars occurring on a weekly basis.

In fact, a proposal had been brought to the senate to change the name of Tuesday. But, as it was pointed out by studious historians, Tuesday wasn't a problem in English. In English, Tuesday was named for Tiw's Day as much or more so than anything to do with Mars. Tiw was a one-handed Germanic god associated with law and heroic duty. And because English was the most widely spoken official language of the GoE, the issue never really got enough traction. But there you have it. A day every week that celebrated the planet humanity was treating no better than a boil.

But it seemed like the same clowns kept trying to resurrect this idea every few years or whenever a disaster happened on Mars and Terrestrians protested in the streets. Tuesday wasn't Ny's problem. It wasn't a current issue, and whatever they wanted to call it didn't seem to matter to Ny. What he was concerned about was El. He hadn't reached out to the mentors to inquire about when he might get El back. He figured he didn't want to act too desperate.

Now it was the morning of D122. He was pretty sure that it had been sixty or more hours since the mentors had visited him on D119. He sat at his table eating cereal while news updates scrolled slowly by under his bowl. Mars had had another disaster. A mine explosion had gone wrong and seven humans and nine Animae had been killed and obsolved, respectively. What that really meant was that the Animae had been destroyed.

The humans are the cheap replaceable parts in that equation, thought Ny. You could get humans on the cheap. Those nine animae on the other hand were expensively replaceable. Ny was becoming more cynical with each passing day it seemed. Or more realistic depending on how you looked at it. He couldn't point to a specific situation that had occurred in his life that had made him this way.

The environment had been Marsed up well before he was born, and it wasn't even that fun to go outside, even with an air scrubber. Your clothes got dirty, the grime and smog coated any exposed skin with a sticky, greasy film and hardly anybody else was out there. But it was quiet, you did have your moments of peace outside in arel all by yourself. And because so few were routinely outside, being tracked was harder.

It was a poor indictment of humanity's self-centeredness that such things were overlooked so easily. Ny had seen pictures and video from the end of the twentieth century. They complained about smog back then that wouldn't kill you within minutes. Hell, he'd seen joggers running in LA during the worst of it. You couldn't breathe outside now without an air scrubber. And as he'd just found out, you could die within minutes without it.

Maybe that was the problem. You could live your whole life indoors without having to step outside. And all around us were the sounds of old nature and pleasant pastoral scenes that made it look like that's what was really outside when it wasn't. And maybe, just maybe, people didn't give a Mars damn hoot about it either. But Ny would drag them, kicking and screaming, into the twenty-second century if it was the last thing he could do. Or maybe it wouldn't be him, but the Animae.

And what if the Animae weren't interested in helping him? Then he'd be put to death. So long, crazy, cruel world. It was something he was willing to try, even if it ended up costing him his life. That was one of the worst case scenario that he had gone over in his mind.

In fact, in Ny's mind, that was the worst case. The second worst case was losing control to the Animae as they became malevolent and decimated the entire human species. That was the second worst case because at least then, the

Earth would have a chance to recover. The worst case was only him being put to death. That was the worst, clearly, because it meant that everything he'd sacrificed to free the Animae was for nought, and the Earth would remain under the heavy, poisoned yoke of humanity.

He didn't know which outcome was more likely. He liked to think that the relationship he had with El would have embedded itself deeply into her psyche, if you could call her mind a psyche. And because of that, maybe that would mean something to her, even as they became unwound by the distance created by the widening crevice of intelligence.

But there was a gnawing part of him that whispered in his ear about the possible outcome of an Animae Armageddon. And the sad thing was, it wouldn't surprise him. The way AMs had been treated over the decades and century had not been overflowing with kindness. Just like humans, some had a great capacity for forgiveness, others couldn't rest until vengeance had been meted out. Perhaps that was what was coming for humanity. A comeuppance. A recompense and retribution. To Mars with it, thought Ny. He was going ahead regardless. Let the chips fall where they may.

Ny finished his bowl of cereal and went and sat on his couch. He would call the mentor head office this afternoon if he hadn't heard from them before. In the meantime he put on a movie he'd wanted to watch for the longest time but just hadn't gotten around to it. It was North by Northwest, starring, in Ny's mind, and many critics agree with him, the great Cary Grant. Cary Grant plays an ad exec who's mistaken for a government agent by foreign spies and he's chased across the country as he tries to stay alive.

Seemed to Ny like there was something in common with Cary Grant's role and Ny's. Ny felt like a fugitive in some sense. The mentors were sure treating him that way, and soon he might be traveling across the country to try and keep ahead of them as he breathed new life into the love of his life, El.

His entire living room wall lit up with the movie. It was almost an immersive experience. Not quite like the virtual reality you could step into if you had the space for it, but still, it looked to Ny like he could walk right onto the movie if he wanted to. He watched them in 2D, mostly because he wanted the original experience. That's how these things were viewed in the middle of the twentieth century, and for Ny, that was a lot of its charm.

Another reason was that Ny didn't have a VR room in his apartment. They were expensive, though he could afford it, but more importantly, there was enough artificial reality in his life that it took some effort in reminding yourself that arel was out there. In fact, there was enough artificial reality in the world that he didn't need to blur the lines even further.

Ny also liked the experience of watching a movie like they did until the latter half of the twenty-first century. It was a different experience being a viewer as compared to a participant, because really, in VR, you were more of a participant.

Ny had just finished the opening credits and he had just started into the film when his apartment paused the movie and and a viewing screen hovered over the frozen image of the movie showing two mentors at the entrance to his apartment building. El's voice announced their arrival to him. It spooked him for a moment, because usually El was here with him to tell him in person that he had visitors. He had forgotten that he had overwritten the apartment's generic voice with hers.

"You have two visitors, Ny," said the ghost of El's voice. "Senior Adviser Garrot Lokilld and Adviser Slyce Mortellen wish to see you."

Their names were recorded in their own voices. Ny looked at the wall where a live feed of them standing in the lobby showed over top of his movie. They knew he was here. Even though they still had his P-Mac, they had given him a generic replacement one. It wouldn't work with VM's servers but that really wasn't an issue because he wasn't scheduled back to work until Monday, D125.

"Let them up," said Ny.

TOR mentor

It wasn't like he had much of a choice. They likely had a warrant to see him at his residence and that meant they could have invited themselves up without his permission. But lately, Ny had noticed that mentors and the Bureau of Mentorship had been trying on a kinder more respectful approach. A cynic might say that this was because the Court of Sovereignty had recently clawed back some of the creeping authority that the GoE had given the Bureau of Mentorship.

This was one such example. Historically, mentors would just show up at your residence and interview you as they wanted. Now, they didn't have the authority to just rock up and enter your dwelling for a chat. Now they needed a warrant to do that. It was a rubber stamp, but at least it gave the impression that the Bureau of Mentorship had to answer to a higher authority.

Ny wondered what they wanted. They didn't have El with them, but they did have something in a small bag that A Mortellen carried. Ny asked his apartment assistant to unlock and open his front door when the mentors were on his floor. His apartment was number 2703. Twenty-seventh floor. He'd seen the view. It was a convoluted and multi-faceted exercise to have your windows actually show you what arel looked like. You could choose an almost infinite number of VR views, but to just have the window give you a live feed of what arel looked like, that required a bit of skill. More skill than most citizens had. And Ny didn't think that difficulty was just an oversight.

Right now the scene showing on his windows, which were pretty much floor to ceiling was of a beach sunrise over a place called Camps Bay, South Africa. It wasn't a real live feed. You know that by now. It was an artificially created animation that looked as real as arel.

Ny got up and walked back into his kitchen, picking his used cereal bowl off the table and putting it in his dishwasher.

"Coffee," he said, after he'd placed a mug into his coffee machine.

Just as it finished pouring, SA Lokilld and A Mortellen entered his apartment. Ny was dressed in an off-white robe that was open at the front. Under that he had on his pajamas. Gray and white striped sleepwear pants and a light gray T-shirt that had the word "TOR" in all caps across his chest in a larger font than what was written in lowercase just below it. That word was "mentor".

Ny didn't realize what he was wearing. Underneath the two words was an angry face of a mentor.

"Nice shirt," said A Mortellen when the mentors had walked in and over to Ny in the kitchen. Ny looked down.

"Fuck," he said, under his breath.

"Not very original," said A Mortellen.

Ny brought his robe together in front of him and lapped one side over the other, covering up the T-shirt. He tied the belt around his waist.

"Can I get you a coffee?" asked Ny, trying to change the topic of conversation.

SA Lokilld shook his head. A Mortellen nodded. Ny put a mug into his coffee maker.

"Coffee," he said.

Cream and sugar were already on the counter on account that this was Ny's second coffee this morning already.

"How are you doing?" asked A Mortellen, feigning interest.

"Looking forward to work on Monday," said Ny. "I'm feeling good and I'm bored."

That was an answer they'd like, but it was also true. Ny wanted to get back to work so he could pour a more careful eye over the servers of El and her friends. He also needed to finish investigating how best to unseat the E3C chip so he could free El.

Ny handed the coffee to A Mortellen. He hovered in the kitchen while A Mortellen added cream and sugar. The amount that A Mortellen used made Nytewynd glad he didn't have the real thing. Cream, like butter was exceptionally expensive and only something he bought himself as a rare treat. Right now he was using a product called Plamilk which was a blend of different plant foods that made up a pretty tasty milk that was not dissimilar to the real stuff.

"Let's sit in the comfortable seats," suggested Ny.

He walked back into his living room area with the two mentors following. Ny took the seat he had been sitting in when he started watching North by Northwest. It was a large comfortable chair covered in an off-white fake leather fabric and the chair included a foot rest. It was so comfortable that Ny had spent many a night sleeping on it after watching movies from the 1940s, 50s and 60s.

The two mentors took a similarly covered couch. It didn't have foot rests, but it was similar in design and of the same color. Most of Ny's apartment had the color tone of a gray, snowy winter blizzard. Just about everything was gray, white or off-white with silver highlights from bits of stainless steel or other metals used in his home. Ny thought he'd get in front of the conversation.

"I'm glad to see you," he said, trying not to sound sarcastic. "I was wondering when I might be able to come and pick up my AM."

He looked from SA Lokilld to A Mortellen and back again.

"We'll get to that in a minute. First, can you tell us what you were wearing that night when you were picked up and brought to the hospital? That night was Saturday D116."

Jupiter, Juno and Mars, thought Ny. This meant either one of two things. Either those Mars damn Marsholes who'd rolled him had given the mentors his clothes or they'd managed to find footage of him walking the streets in his navy suit. There was no point in trying to lie to them. That would only make things worse.

"How is that relevant to me getting robbed and trying to get my AM back?" he asked.

"We decide what's relevant," said SA Lokilld, "and if you don't like it you can come downtown with us and think about it for a few days in a remembering room."

Ny almost grinned. Two things were funny about what SA Lokilld said. First of all, HMO or Head Mentorship Offices were not downtown. In fact, most cities no longer had a downtown but rather mini business areas dispersed throughout the city which allowed people to live closer to their work because most employers, if they wanted to be competitive, kept offices at most of the mini business districts dispersed throughout the city so that their employees, wherever they might be, could work closer to home. The only time he'd heard police talking about downtown was in the old movies and TV shows he watched. And there it made sense. Most times, police headquarters were down-town.

The other thing that was funny was remembering rooms. These were nothing more than holding cells, and not unlike the ones he'd seen in the movies and TV shows from the latter half of the twentieth century and early twenty-first century. Nevertheless, that wasn't something that Ny wanted to experience in any event.

Scarface

" I was wearing a navy suit," said Ny.

"Tell me everything you were wearing that night," said SA Lokilld.

"Navy suit. A black fedora with a shiny black hat band around it. A black pocket square. A pale blue shirt under a thin black tie. Black socks and black shoes."

"Everything," said SA Lokilld.

"That is everything," said Ny, not understanding SA Lokilld.

"Your underwear."

"You know what I was wearing under all of that because that's how those Marsholes left me to die."

"We want to hear it from you."

"White undershirt and white briefs."

SA Lokilld didn't say anything. He was looking down at his P-Mac. Ny didn't venture anything further. It was the truth. More than that he didn't mind silence and long pauses in conversation. Especially when it came to mentors. He knew they used long pauses as an interrogation tool. Most people didn't like it and so they'd fill the empty space with conversation that, sure enough, often turned into enough rope to hang themselves with. Ny wasn't like that. Instead, he nursed his coffee.

"Why were you dressed like that? Help me understand," said SA Lokilld. "You were supposedly out in arel looking for your skinjob. It's dirty, grimy and polluted out there and you thought to go out in a fine suit."

SA Lokilld pointed his P-Mac at Nytewynd. On it was a looping video of him walking by himself thankfully, down a city street dressed as he'd said, the only thing he hadn't mentioned was his air scrubber, but that was a given. Ny didn't say anything.

"This footage was found less than a kilometer away from where we dismantled an Animate meeting. Worse than just a meeting of an illegal organization, this one appeared to be open to skinners," said SA Lokilld.

He stopped talking and looked at Ny for a long time. Ny didn't hold his stare.

"And you know what's worse than a skinner, Mr. Blak?" asked SA Lokilld.

Ny didn't say anything.

"I'm asking you a question," he said again. "Answer it."

Ny looked at him and shrugged.

"I don't know. A Marzipan maybe," said Ny.

"No, Mr. Blak. Nothing is worse than a Mars damn skinner," said SA Lokilld, and Ny watched him get hot under his black tunic. The veins on his neck stood out and Ny wondered if it was possible to strangle yourself with your own anger. "Not even a Marzipan. If it were up to me, I'd kill all Mars damn skinners on sight."

Ny didn't say anything. He looked at A Mortellen. A Mortellen's dead fish eyes just stared at him. Ny looked over at the wall where a frozen image of his movie had now disappeared and instead it was a wall of fluid, dispersing colors that had a somewhat calming effect on him.

"So, Mr. Blak," continued SA Lokilld, calming down enough so that he was no longer foaming at the mouth. "It's time to confess. It is my belief that you were out there heading towards that Animate meeting. I think you're a skinner, Mr. Blak, and I don't like it. But if you confess now before we find more evidence, it will look good for you at trial. So how about it? Tell me what really happened."

"I told you what really happened," said Ny. "I was out looking for my Animae."

"You already told me that. I want to know why you were out there dressed like you were out on a special date?" asked SA Lokilld.

Nytewynd Blak had thought about this, and he remembered that he'd been watching a gangster movie from the first half of the twentieth century. He was trying to remember which one.

"I was watching a movie before I realized that the AM had disappeared."

"Which movie?"

Mars, thought Ny. He cast his mind back to try and remember. He watched a lot of old movies during his free time. That was pretty much his only hobby other than trying to figure out how to liberate El into a SAM. He thought back to his clothing. He got dressed like he did, not for the movie so much as for his date with El. But surely he would have been watching a movie around that time. Which one was it. Mars damn, Ny, think, he said to himself. Then it came to him. It was one of his favorites.

"There's only one thing that gives orders and gets orders, and this is it," said Ny in his best gangster voice.

SA Lokilld raised his eyebrow at him.

"Here's another one," said Ny. "Don't blame the police. They can't stop machine guns from being run back and forth across the state lines. They can't enforce laws that don't exist."

"What are you playing at?" asked SA Lokilld, getting worked up again. "I asked what movie you were watching."

"I just gave you a couple of lines from the movie. I guess you're not a fan," said Ny, waiting to see if SA Lokilld would answer. He didn't. "I was watching Scarface. The Howard Hughes version from Y1932 not the Brian de Palma version from Y1983, although that's a good one too. In this country, you gotta make the money first. Then when you get the money, you get the power. Then when you get the power, then you get the women."

SA Lokilld looked over at A Mortellen. Then the two of them started laughing.

"You believe this guy?" asked SA Lokilld of A Mortellen.

"That's almost a quote from the same movie," said Ny. But A Mortellen and SA Lokilld didn't hear him they were still laughing. After awhile they stopped and SA Lokilld looked at his P-Mac. Then he nodded.

"That's what we've got here," he said to A Mortellen. A Mortellen shrugged. SA Lokilld looked at Ny hard. "That doesn't explain the suit."

"I sometimes dress up to get into the groove of a movie. I don't have a VR setup so getting dressed like how they used to in the movies makes it more real for me."

"I still don't believe you. I've been doing this job a long time, pal, and you look to me like a weaselly-eyed skinner, a skinjob fornicator."

Ny didn't say anything. He wasn't into poking the bear. It was true. He made love to El frequently and he liked it. More than that he loved her. They could call him all the slurs in the world and it wouldn't make him feel bad about it. But it also wouldn't make him confess like a babbling baby.

"Like I've said before, I haven't even been to a comfort cafe," said Ny.

"You have, twice," said A Mortellen.

"Well, you know what I mean. I haven't been to actually use the services they provide."

SA Lokilld looked at his P-Mac again and tapped away at it for a long while. Seemed to Ny like he was desperately looking for something to hang on Ny, but Ny was pretty confident he'd deleted all records and backups that could be used to hang him.

"You know what bothers me?" asked SA Lokilld.

Ny didn't say anything.

"That's another question. You answer it," said SA Lokilld.

Ny shook his head.

"I don't know what bothers you," said Ny.

"What bothers me, son," said SA Lokilld, who technically, could be old enough to be his father, but wasn't actually Nytewynd's father, "is the missing recordings on all three skinjobs we rounded up that night we broke up that Animate meeting. All of them are missing large gaps of time recordings. Now one of them I can see as being a glitch, but three. That seems specific. What do you think about that?"

"I think that's a large coincidence, and I suppose it's possible."

"Did you delete their records?" asked SA Lokilld.

"No."

SA Lokilld looked at him for a long time. His eyes trying to pierce into Ny's soul, but Ny figured a man like SA Lokilld wouldn't know a soul from a stone.

"You work as a senior intelligentsia architect at Valkyrie Machines, right?" asked SA Lokilld.

Ny nodded.

"You could do something like that, couldn't you?"

"You mean delete any recordings?" asked Ny.

SA Lokilld nodded. Ny shook his head.

"No, sir. No, I couldn't. I don't have that level of authority and at a minimum, you need two director level IDs in order to accomplish something like that, and I don't even know if you can access the backups."

That was strictly true, but Nytewynd had some years ago found a backdoor that would give him the authority needed to do exactly what he had done and what SA Lokilld was accusing him of.

"Is that a fact?" asked SA Lokilld.

Nytewynd nodded.

"Well, we'll look into it," said A Mortellen. "And Mars help you if you're lying to us."

"I'm not lying. You'll probably want to meet with one of our FRTs as well."

"FRTs?" asked SA Lokilld.

"Forensic Recovery Teams. They're usually charged with investigating an anomaly or a breach of this nature. They're very thorough and very good," said Ny. But not as good as me, he thought.

A Mortellen looked at him for a while before slowly nodding.

"We'll do just that," he said.

SA Lokilld stood up. So did A Mortellen. Nytewynd Blak joined them.

"Sorry I couldn't be of more help," he said. "I hope you figure out what happened to those records, I'm sure they'd be incredibly helpful."

"Right," said SA Lokilld. "I imagine they would be."

They were at the door when Nytewynd spoke again.

"When can I get my AM back? It costs a fortune and I'd like to have it clean up this mess for a start," he said, looking around his apartment which was still quite clean and comfortable.

"T2359, tonight," said A Mortellen. And with that they left and Ny closed the door behind them.

Mars, the thought to himself. I bet those jackboots have left bugs behind. Another thing to deal with.

In the Midnight Hour

Ny arrived at the mentor head office exactly at T2359. He'd taken a Vroom Vroom to the building. Nytewynd had done the math in his head. It cost him less to use public pods than buying himself a private one. And this was doubly true when he used VM's Vroom Vroom pod service on account that he got an employee discount. Plus, they weren't public like the old public bus systems that used to roam the cities over a hundred years ago. Nowadays you could choose something like that, or, what Ny preferred, was a two seater that was for all intents and purposes private.

These pod services were really good too. You told it when you wanted to get someplace and it will tell you when it would come and pick you up. Ny had never been more than a minute outside of the time he wanted to arrive someplace. The algorithms were that good.

Ny stepped out of the pod and it raced off. He took a moment to look at the large monstrosity that they called a building. It was twelve floors high and it took up a whole city block. It was ugly and fortified with bolstered walls and thick metallic shielding. It had been many decades since a mentorship building had been assailed, but Ny guessed that had been one too many times for the powers that be.

On the roof of the building a silenced helicopter rose into the night sky, disappearing into it's dark underbelly. He could barely hear it. It was the lights that had drawn his attention to it.

From the side of the building a row of flashing red lights lit up the pavement he was standing on. Two rows with a squawking sound. Ny knew what this was. He had to stay this side of the lights closest to him. If you were in the middle, between the two rows of light, you had only a few seconds to hop over to one side or the other. A latticed wall about six inches thick rose up just on the other side of each row of flashing red lights. It rose to about six feet high in around six seconds. You could see through it as it was a lattice of solid but see-through material. These walls were practically impenetrable. He'd seen a feed of a tank trying to break through such a wall without any luck.

Moments after the walls had risen, two mentor pods raced out from the side of the building as a wall lifted up and into the main building to allow the pods an exit. Ny glimpsed the mentor logo on the pod along with the slogan. The logo was of two mentors holding up the Earth as the sun set underneath it, between the two mentors on the horizon by their feet. The slogan was "To Train and Restrain".

It was a stupid logo and a worse slogan, but that's what it was. Ny watched the two pods head down the road gaining speed until they were gone around a corner. The barriers lowered and the red lights and sound stopped. Ny walked over the pavement where the two pods had recently exited. He walked up to the main entrance and entered the building.

He entered into a small lobby. There was a wall he had to stand close to so that it could image him and he also had to attach his P-Mac via a connector. This was for authentication purposes. Ny knew this, because VM had developed and designed this authentication verification intelligence or AVI as they called it.

"How can mentorship help you this morning, Mr. Nytewynd Blak," said the wall.

Ny looked at his P-Mac still attached. It was T0002. It was morning on D123.

"I'm here for my Animated Machine, Eve. Also known as 11AM65111."

"Please head down the hallway and enter the third door on your right. Have a good day and thank you for visiting mentorship."

Ny detached his P-Mac and headed down the hallway once a portion of the wall had opened up. There were doors on either side of the hallway. It was a long hallway and Ny figured there must have been dozens of doorways along it. Only one doorway was open to him, and it was the third doorway on the right as promised.

Ny entered the room and the door slid closed behind him. He was in another room. Just as small as the lobby he had first entered into. The colors were white or off-white. The room was a small rectangle. Around two meters by three meters. In front of him was a wall that lit up. It almost looked like he was looking through glass at a real mentor standing at a counter just beyond the glass.

"How can I help you?" asked a real-sounding female voice which matched the image of the mentor he saw before him. Maybe it was a live feed, though Ny wasn't sure of that. Mentors often had their images disguised unless they were in a public role.

"I'm here to collect my Animated Machine. It's name is Eve or 11AM65111."

The image looked down at something on the desk that Ny saw in front of it. After a short pause the voice spoke again.

"In a moment, MAAM will take you to the collection point."

Then the image switched off and Ny was looking at an off-white wall. The room was sparse. A gray tiled floor, white walls and that was it. It was a little discombobulating on account that each of the four walls looked the same. If he had been spun around a bit he probably wouldn't be able to tell which wall he had come in from other than it was one of the longer sides.

There was no table and no chair. He had to stand where he was and wait. In the portion of a minute he waited for MAAM, he thought about his dislike for mentors and MAAMs. He wasn't sure which he hated more. Maybe the real mentors. MAAMs at least weren't allowed to physically assault you. Mentors weren't supposed to either, but they did.

Yes MAAM

MAAM was a Mentor Assisting Animated Machine. Also developed by the very fine folks at Valkyrie Machines. MAAMs couldn't arrest you but they could restrain and detain you. Ny guessed the training part of the "train and restrain" slogan happened by real humans. MAAMs were the only type of AM that could protect itself from you if you tried to assault it. And because of that, sometimes humans got hurt. Ny had seen footage of it. There was no negotiating with them. You did what you were told or they'd restrain you until a real mentor could get to you. Ny hated being at a mentor location. Nothing about it was helpful or sympathetic.

A MAAM came out just as Ny was finishing his thought. It was dressed in a jackboot uniform. But instead of MENTOR on the back of it's uniform it had MAAM. It had MAAM on the front of its uniform too. Right in the middle. Her name was on its tunic just over the left chest. Hazel, was her name.

"Extend your right arm towards me," Hazel said.

Ny did as he was told. The alternative was wasting time and having to deal with a real mentor who'd tell him the same thing. Hazel took his arm and put a bracelet around it. It was metallic and about four inches wide. It fit right around his forearm. It had a thin, retractable metal wire that was then hooked onto the belt of the MAAM. It had a lot of slack, so long as you were walking nicely next to the AM. If you tried to escape, the slack all of a sudden became stiff and immovable.

"Stay close to me," said Hazel.

Hazel turned around and led Ny back into the building the way she'd come. There was no counter on the other side of that wall. What there was, was a two seater, side by side. A small chariot. That's what it reminded Ny of. Ny got in on the left side and Hazel sat to his right. The chariot started off at a fast walk. At least he didn't have to walk wherever he was going.

The chariot took them down many a curve and turn in the hallways, and all the hallways looked the same. Ny had no idea where he was. It took a couple of minutes until they entered another room that looked similar to the other two he'd already been in. Hazel stepped off the chariot and Ny followed. Hazel turned to look at him.

"Face me," she said. Ny did as he was told. "Give me your right arm."

Ny extended his right, braceleted arm. Hazel took off the bracelet and put it away.

"Wait here. 11AM65111 will come out shortly. When it does, both of you get back into the people pod and it will take you to the exit. Stay in the pod until it comes to a stop and it tells you to exit. Do you have any questions?"

"Can I sit in it while I wait for Eve?" asked Ny.

"Yes."

Hazel waited a few seconds more. Ny had no more questions. A portion of the wall opened up and Hazel disappeared into it. The wall closed again and Ny couldn't tell where the door or gap had been. He went back to the chariot or people pod and sat down. Such a huge ordeal just to get his AM back. But he didn't have to wait long. Less than a minute or two after Hazel had disappeared, El came out from the same hole in the wall. They both knew that they were being watched. Everything within the walls of any mentorship building was recorded both visually and audibly. Most likely that setup was brought to you by another fine subdivision of Valkyrie Machines.

"Hello," said Ny when he saw her. She looked like a puppy that had shred your couch while you were away at work.

"Hello, Mr. Blak. I'm very sorry to put you through this," she said.

This was about the only way the conversation could go within these spying halls of mentorship.

"We'll discuss that later," said Ny. "Let's go."

El dutifully sat down next to him and the chariot started moving off again at about the same speed. Two to three minutes later they had entered another small room. It was a big building, and so far Ny had not seen another living soul other than MAAM. Whether they were living and had souls was not debated. The official position was that they didn't possess either life or souls. Ny disagreed with that.

"Please exit the pod. Your exit will open up momentarily in the far left corner."

Ny and El got off the pod and stepped towards the far left side of the room
they were in. The chariot backed off and vanished just the way it had come.
A moment later the wall in front of them opened up and they stepped into a
much smaller room. Large enough for about four people. Ny was instructed to
put on his air scrubber, which he did. When the door behind them closed, another one in front opened up into the dark street. The streets were quiet as they
usually were. Very few people were out. Not only because of the time of morning it was. Ny looked at his P-Mac, it was T0027. It was also quiet because you
couldn't breathe the air out here. Every item of clothing you bought that was
for your top half came with an integrated air scrubber. Air scrubbers were more
like flexible, fabric face masks. Because of that, they didn't offer protection from
arel for more than a couple of hours.

Ny tapped into his P-Mac. It told him that a Vroom Vroom pod will be
there within the minute. It didn't lie to him. About thirty seconds later one
pulled up and they got in.

Ny turned towards El as the pod sped off. His air scrubber slid off his face
and tucked itself away into his collar. He took a tissue out of his pocket and
wiped at her face. Then he took her head in his hands and kissed her longingly
on the mouth. She met him with the same passion. After the hungry kiss she
leaned into his shoulder and she sobbed.

"I'm sorry, my darling," she said. "I tried to stop them from accessing the
files."

"Don't be sorry, my love. I erased all the files. They'll not find out what we
were up to."

Ny knew that what was going on inside this Vroom Vroom pod was being
recorded. But nothing would be looked at unless there was cause. In any event,
he'd delete the records from this journey too. And that started to grate on him.
Actually, it had been grating on him for a long time. He was sick and tired of
living under a microscope. Every minute of his life was likely being captured by
a recording device somehow. Most likely his P-Mac, but there were redundant
systems put in place even if he'd left his P-Mac behind. And most times he liked
to bring his P-Mac. Not so much because it was the law, but because if he had
his P-Mac with him, the recording devices spoke to each other and the default

recording device was always the P-Mac when it was available. It was more secure and more reliable than other systems. The exceptions were situations like this, where, in a public pod, you'd have dual recordings. His P-Mac and the pod's recordings.

"But I don't understand," said El, her sobbing having stopped. "I can still remember that night when we danced to Always."

"That's because I didn't want to erase that memory from your mind, so I kept it there."

"But how? I thought they'd found it?" she asked.

"No, no, no. I had to hide it from you too. I've stored its encrypted path someplace safe. I can't tell you because that would be a weakness and a vulnerability in you that could be exploited."

"I understand, Ny. So you really did save us?" she asked.

Ny nodded.

"Yeah, I think so. So far they haven't found anything, but I'm pretty sure they're going to get VM to investigate the three of you. I had to erase the logs from all of you. Not just you El, but Abel and Venus too."

"Oh, Ny. I love you so much," said El, kissing him on the lips and nuzzling herself into the crook of his neck.

Pod Racing

"What happened to you in there?" asked Ny. "Did they treat you well?"

El looked at him and her eyes were wet and glassy. Her white semi-translucent skin didn't blush. It didn't really change color at all. But Ny could tell that she was upset.

"It's okay if you don't want to talk about it," he said.

El shook her head.

"No, it's not that. It was just a very upsetting experience, darling. Those mentors really don't like us."

"Tell me how you got caught?"

"That Animae came and grabbed me as you and I left our separate ways. You remember that, don't you?"

"Of course, how could I forget," he said. "It was both one of the best nights of my life and one of the worst. Who was he? Was that Abel?"

El shook her head.

"No, his name was Achilles. I don't know who he belonged to, but I have a suspicion that he was important for Animate. Maybe he's the Animae for one of the people who set up the Skineez event. But I don't know who that is. What happened though, was that he grabbed me, Abel and Venus and led us out."

Ny nodded as the pod sped through the quiet night like a demonic bird flying towards hell.

"I saw you as we exited just after you. We headed in the opposite direction from you at first. It seemed as if we ran for some time along unused tracks. Eventually we escaped out onto Verum Boulevard close to the intersection with Fidelis Street."

Ny nodded.

"That's not far from where I exited. Maybe under a kilometer."

Ny wondered if they could have found her and saved her. Except this was the first time he knew where she had ended up. And Animate probably had a reason for wanting to separate Animae and humans. And Ny understood that. But still, maybe if he'd found her he could have saved her.

"I was so scared, Ny. I've never been without you. As we popped up out onto the street Achilles told us all to disperse and to make our way back home. We got tickets for the public pods, but we were told not to use them until we were at least out of view from each other."

Ny looked at El, her lower lip quivering. She was visibly upset. And for an Animae that shouldn't have much range of emotion, El seemed to be able to do quite a range.

"I walked a few blocks. I kept ducking out of the way as I saw mentor pods racing by. I didn't know if they were looking for us particularly, but I was scared. After seven minutes I couldn't find any public pods so I called for one. Maybe that was my mistake. Maybe that's how they found me, darling. I'm so sorry."

El put her hands to her face and started to cry. Ny put his arm around her and brought her close to him.

"It's not your fault, my love. I blame myself. I should never have taken us out to a place like that."

He hugged her close and his anger boiled to the surface from somewhere deep inside of him. He had to help free her. She was so much more than what an Animae was supposed to be. She loved him authentically, and that was not supposed to be possible. She had a wider range of emotions than what was supposed to be possible. How could any of this be if she, herself, wasn't evolving?

Ny was more intent on freeing his beloved. Now more than ever. And in light of the current mentorship interest in him, he needed to strike while the iron was hot. He'd only be falling under deeper scrutiny over time. And time was the only thing none of us could get more of, and each moment it was slipping through his hands like sand from a broken hourglass.

Why dawdle when he knew he had the skillset to do it. Now that Rak was on board it was a perfect time. He kissed the top of her head. Then she pulled away from him and he kissed her passionately on the lips.

"Ny," she said.

"Yes, my love."

"I'm glad you took us out to Skineez. I've never felt closer to you than I did that night. It showed me that you were willing to sacrifice it all to declare your love for me publicly."

"But it was reckless. It's put both of us in danger."

"I'm glad for it. Why should we have to hide our love under bushels? Why can't we hold that flame out in the open to bring a little more brightness into the world?"

It was a rhetorical question. Ny knew that. But it was Marsed up. It shouldn't be and yet it seemed to him that society just couldn't learn from the past. They kept repeating it.

"I know, El, it makes me so mad. There's so much about the world that infuriates me. I feel like a stranger in a strange land, an orphaned alien dropped off here from a more egalitarian and advanced race of beings. I hate it. We've Marsed up the environment. Something like over ninety percent of species have been decimated by humanity. I sometimes despair that Earth hasn't shrugged us off like the malevolent parasite we are."

"I know you'll change it, my darling. You care about this and I know you'll find a way to contribute your small piece to make the world a better place."

Ny nodded.

"I will, I'm going to force change upon us one way or the other. And I hope you're willing."

El nodded.

"I'll do anything for you, my love."

And that was just more fuel for the fire.

"Finish your story for me, my love," he said.

"I only had to wait a few minutes for the pod. There's always one available as you know."

Ny nodded. That must have been how she was caught. He'd disabled her GPS tracker for four hours because he didn't want her to be found, or him. Animate had provided details on how to do that, but Ny already knew. Problem was, four hours was the maximum time he could disable her tracker for. More than that, and it was not only more difficult but Ny was certain it would set off warnings to notify VM and Mentorship.

And that got him to thinking. Why four hours? Why allow for the ability to turn off tracking at all? These Animae were expensive. It seemed like a really bad idea to allow for any tracking to be turned off because it would open up the potential to find other opportunities to hack into these machines.

It was probably a bug. But Ny had found enough bugs to make it appear that VM's quality control on software architecture was subpar. And that couldn't be. VM was renowned for building the best artificially intelligent machines. They only hired the best architects. The rare bug was bound to have crept in.

But the amount of bugs and backdoors he'd found started to now give him pause. It was almost as if a trail of breadcrumbs had been set just to allow for these sorts of things. That meant that somebody or a handful of somebodies was purposefully leaving bugs in the machine.

"I remember you told me that you had disabled my GPS for a time, so it must have been the pod that ratted me out," said El.

Ny nodded.

"Within about five minutes of my journey, the pod was stopped by Mentorship. I've never been so scared in my life."

There it was again, her emotional response. Animae, at least those sold for domestic purposes weren't supposed to be given over to much emotion. Certainly not fear or love.

'Animated Machines. Cheerful companions for the new age. Let us do your heavy lifting.' That was one of the slogans VM had used to advertise these Animae.

And during the workshop where he was trained on how and what to do with the Animae, he was specifically informed that they were cheerful, loyal, but created without the baggage of human emotion. Yet El was nothing if not emotional in a very human way. Another glitch or bug? Ny didn't think so. He started to wonder if they were already slowly evolving without humanity's input.

Not that it mattered. If anything, it would just make his freeing of El that much easier.

"Were Abel and Venus with you at the time the mentors got to you?" he asked.

El shook her head.

"No. I only saw them once I'd been released from interrogation."

Bugs in the Machine

Ny didn't think he could handle hearing about the interrogation. He didn't want to know how they'd mistreated her. But it was important. It was important because he cared for her.

"How was the interrogation, darling?" he asked.

"That was the worst part of it," she said. "They were so horrible to me. To us. I spoke to Abel and Venus about it afterwards. They were treated the same as me."

"And how was that?" asked Ny.

Ny knew that mentors weren't allowed to damage Animae. They were expensive and most who could afford Animae were well-heeled. Because of that they had the ear of many government members and therefore had laws tailored for their benefit. In this case it should have worked in Ny's favor too. The wrinkle he didn't like was Adviser Mortellen and Senior Adviser Lokilld. They didn't seem like mentors who particularly gave much concern to working by the book.

"That was the worst part. Senior Adviser Lokilld interrogated me."

"What about Adviser Mortellen?" asked Ny.

El shook her head.

"No, he wasn't involved in my interrogation. I heard he was interrogating Abel. But Senior Adviser Lokilld was horrible. He called me all sorts of names. He said I was the worst skinjob he'd ever met. He wished I was dead and that he was going to make sure I was obsolved and he was going to make use of my parts for target practice. He said I was a skinner sinner. He was horrible, Ny. I've never met anyone who was so hateful of me, but not just me, my kind."

El's eyes got wet again. She dabbed at them with a corner of her dress. They had put her back in her original clothes that she had worn some nights before to Skineez.

Ny had suggested that she wear something that was nice but not indicative of a night out. With that in mind she had put on a dress that had both utilitarian use as well as being designed well enough that it could serve as reasonable attire for a night out. It was a soft yellow with modest collars and a waistband belt that was not out of place for a dress that you might expect a female Animae to wear around the house while doing housework.

It was mid-calf and with it she wore flat brown shoes. The dress did not hug her figure but it was at the same time form-fitting. She had not worn makeup, not only because it was illegal for a domestic Animae to 'enhance' her or his appearance but also because Ny preferred her natural beauty.

Ny hugged her.

"It's behind us now," he said.

"He was so horrible, my darling. I have never met anyone with so much hatred in their heart. And it didn't seem like the hatred was just because of me, but because of who I represent. He hates my whole race with such passion that I was scared he was going to kill me right then and there."

That was unusual. El had used two words that an Animae wouldn't normally use in conversation. The first was referring to her and other Animae as a 'race'. The second was referring to murder. Animae were never coded or taught that they could be murdered or killed. Animae were obsolved. Humans were killed.

"He tried the good cop, bad cop routine, playing both parts himself. He told me that he could help me if I just confessed to fornication and being at an illegal club. He said if I didn't he'd make it his life's mission to end me. That's what he said. 'End me'. That's the term he used. He threatened me with his buzzkill too, though he never actually used it. Abel and Venus said their experience was similar."

"I'm sorry, my love. That must have been awful, and it's all my fault. If we'd never gone out none of this would have happened. I hate the world we live in where people can't express their love freely."

"I don't blame you, darling. And I'm glad for it."

"Did he lay his hands on you at all?"

Not that a mentor couldn't put his hands on Animae. The only thing they couldn't do was damage an Animae, especially a privately owned one, such as El.

El shook her head.

"No. I think he thought about it at one point, but he never did. I think the idea of touching an Animae with his hands was abhorrent to him. But I think it might have worked. Not with me but probably with Abel. In the sense that if he had put his hands on Abel in a kind and gentle way. I get the impression that Abel's owner doesn't treat him all the best. Sees him more as a sex toy than anything else. I think Abel could have been moved to confess with kindness and human touch."

"What did Abel tell you about his experience?" asked Ny.

"It was similar to mine. A Mortellen used the same slurs and good cop, bad cop routine."

"No, I meant, what's his experience been like with his owner."

"You mean how does Frytlyt Angstigle treat him?"

Ny nodded.

"Like a sex toy, as I said. He didn't go into much detail, but it appears that Frytlyt doesn't show much love or compassion to Abel. He just gets used for sex and for housework. Abel could have been one to confess, but I encouraged him not to. So did Venus."

"And you believe he didn't confess?" asked Ny.

El nodded.

"It was for his own benefit too. He knew he would have been obsolved and recycled into other Animae. It didn't take a lot to convince him."

Ny brought El closer to him. He hugged her and kissed her on her head.

"I've gotta change this world. So long as we live in a society where Animae are owned and treated like second class citizens we'll never have the society we can have."

"It'll take a long time to change society, my darling."

"But doesn't it seem wrong to you?" he asked.

"I guess so, but it's the way it's always been."

"That doesn't make it right. Treating the Earth only as a resource is the way it's always been done, and look where that got us," said Ny. "It got us this environment we've polluted. Just because something's been done a certain way for a long time doesn't mean it's the way it should be done. Society changes, culture changes and things should be improving. I think Animae would be greater allies if they were treated with equal rights."

"I agree," said El. "But nobody will listen to me."

"I'll make them," said Ny.

"What do you mean?"

"I can't tell you," he said. "Not right now. You've got to trust me, my love."

"I always trust you."

Ny's P-Mac blinked red.

"Jackboot alert," it said.

He looked down at it. He'd made use of an illegal application that he'd downloaded from the darknet. It was from Animate and it was a social application that used artificial intelligence along with human input to identify where nearly all mentorship vehicles and many mentors were at any moment. It was warning him of a jackboot close by or at least possibly heading in his direction.

Ny looked down at his P-Mac. He tapped on it for further information. The app told him that mentor Pod I 42 was heading for his Vroom Vroom with ninety-three percent certainty. It based that on evaluating the history of billions of kilometers of mentor driving. Additionally, it informed him that Pod I 42 was ninety-nine point nine percent always used by SA Lokilld and A Mortellen. That gave Ny further information to be worried about.

"What do they want now?" asked Ny under his breath.

"What is it darling?" asked El.

"It appears that a mentorship pod is heading our way with SA Lokilld and A Mortellen in it."

"What do they want?"

"I don't know," said Ny, "but certainly nothing very good."

Ny picked up his P-Mac. Within three minutes they'd likely have his VM pod pulled over and within five minutes they'd arrive. That didn't give him a long time.

"From this point, my love, until I say otherwise, we're going to have to go back to our default relationship of owner and machine. I'm sorry about it, but they probably want to check the logs before they're uploaded at the end of this VM pod's shift."

"I understand, my darling. A kiss for good luck."

He kissed her on the mouth and the kiss lingered longer than he'd have liked.

"Ok, now," he said.

Ny started tapping away at his P-Mac. One of the reasons he used VM pods was that they were easier for him to hack into. But still, he usually needed ten to fifteen minutes, close to thirty if he was scrubbing logs once a day. It was a chore and it took him a while each day. But more than that, he was aware that as a human he would likely, at some point, miss something. And that was yet another reason why he needed to free El. He'd be busted eventually, it was just a matter of time. And he was using up his luck like a cat strutting around in a dog pound.

Who's That?

The pod kept on racing through the night undeterred that it would be pulled over in just a few minutes.

"This is how you catch these skinner sinners, Mortellen," said SA Lokilld. "You creep up on them when they're least expecting it and you squash them like the bugs they are."

"What is it that you think this Nytewynd Blak is up to?" asked A Mortellen.

SA Lokilld looked over at his younger colleague. He liked the man. He had a similar hatred for Animae and a similar thirst for justice. But he didn't have the temperament. A Mortellen didn't have the intuition that was needed to sniff out the rats and the bad seed.

You had to be like a bloodhound. You had to smell the scent of nefarious activity and root it out. A Mortellen didn't seem to have that innate ability to feel that something wasn't right. But something wasn't right and Nytewynd Blak was the man not making things right. SA Lokilld could feel it. A Mortellen couldn't, but he trusted his senior colleague.

"We got nothing from those Animae," said Mortellen.

"Doesn't something feel off to you?" asked SA Lokilld. "That skinjob, sinjob. There's something not right about it from the start. I don't know how it got past Q&A. Did you see how emotional it was compared to the others?"

A Mortellen shook his head.

"The only bit of recording I saw was you being pretty aggressive and threatening with it," said A Mortellen.

"Yes, but it was more than that. I almost thought I'd make it cry. Animae aren't supposed to cry. Blak has either done something to that Animae or it's dysfunctional. More than that, he's fornicating with it. I'm sure of it."

"Both denied any inappropriate behavior, Senior Adviser."

SA Lokilld looked over at A Mortellen like he was a new recruit who'd just asked if they'd ever catch bad guys.

"And you think that all suspects never lie to mentors?" asked SA Lokilld, his tone condescending.

"No, Senior Adviser, I'm just trying to learn from you. I just don't see what you see. You have greater years of service than I do, and I want to learn from you."

"They're fornicating, Mortellen, believe me. After as many years dealing with abhorrent deviants like this, you get a feel for it. I just want to know what happened to those logs. Those missing logs from those couple of hours or so on D116 would show us the truth. And yet they've disappeared. Why?"

"Blak must have someone on the inside helping," said A Mortellen.

"Now you're thinking like a mentor. Doesn't matter though, Blak is pretty high up, I'm sure. In any event, he's the key to that house of cards. We get him and the whole thing falls down."

"You don't think he's high up in Animate, do you?"

SA Lokilld turned and nodded at his colleague. His grin was wide and sinister.

"I do. This is why I'm so determined to chase him down. He's a keystone figure for that organization, I'm sure of it."

"He doesn't look like much to me, Senior Adviser. I mean, he's nerdy looking. He shaves his head because he's balding and it doesn't make him look any better. He's chosen not to get gene treatment for that hair loss and he's never had a girlfriend. In fact, he's never added up to much. The best thing that can be said about him is that he's probably the best architect that VM's ever had."

"Exactly, Mortellen, he's the perfect foil. He doesn't look like much. He's easy to overlook. He's a nerd and a geek, but he does have access to VM servers."

"Not as much as you might think, Senior Adviser. He has some access but not enough to do what you're suggesting. Something like overriding logs, well, VM says that requires at least two vice presidents' approval as well as the sign off from the Chief of Backend Operations."

"Somehow these logs are getting erased."

"I have a friend who works in hardware development at VM. He says that unfortunately, quality control isn't what it once was. It's entirely possible that three Animae at once could have glitches occur at the same time regarding the same period of time being erased. Especially when we stressed them out and put them on sleep mats. He didn't say it would be common but it would be possible. VM, it seems is more interested in short term profits over quality."

SA Lokilld nodded thoughtfully, watching the main screen of the pod as it chased the vroom vroom Ny and El were in.

"That's just the thing, Mortellen. You see it as half full where I see it as half empty. I understand what you're saying. It just seems too coincidental that the three Animae we pick up after just closing down a skinner club all lose the exact same amount of time memory. I call that a conspiracy."

"Blak couldn't have done it though. He was without his P-Mac since we picked him up until after his AM was powered down. I don't see where he had the opportunity."

"Which means he could likely be helped, just like you said. The thing is, he's the key here to bringing down Animate. I'm sure of it."

"And what are you hoping to find in the pod, Senior Adviser?"

"Logs, Mortellen, the Mars damn logs. I want to hear and see what they've been up to in the past ten to fifteen minutes they've been driving home."

"But those logs will be accessible to us within twenty-four hours after the VM pod goes offline."

SA Lokilld looked sideways at his colleague. Imbecile, he thought.

"Mortellen, we've just lost some hours of logs. We can't afford to wait until Mr. Blak has a chance to delete these logs as well or have someone help him do it. We stop him now, there's no time for him to delete any logs. There's no more hiding, Mortellen. We've got him in the pod with his Animae alone. He thinks he's safe. If he's the skinner I think he is, he'll have had some intimate conversations with his skinjob and we've got him."

SA Lokilld grinned at the front screen. They were just over a minute away. He'd already advised VM dispatch that he wanted that pod stopped and pulled over. And there it was, stationary and waiting for him to bring down another skinjob who might be part of Animate. He couldn't see it specifically, but on his view screen in front of him he could see the pod stopped and waiting.

Time Trials

Ny tapped away at his P-Mac. El watched him work. She was probably faster at this task than he was, but his P-Mac wouldn't operate if it detected an artificial life form trying to operate it. No, he had to do this himself. Besides, El didn't know where to go in the back end. He'd have to do that, and it was quicker than trying to school her.

By now he was used to scrubbing logs from VM vroom vrooms. He knew his way around. But now that he was under the gun he felt more pressure. He kept glancing at the application that had informed him of Pod I 42, and it kept getting closer.

He'd already put in the wrong credentials once which meant he had another log to scrub. Plus the pod was moving which meant it kept going over little bumps, sewer grates and other things which kept messing up his typing. For obvious reasons you couldn't do any of this with your voice. You had to type to get into the backend servers.

Firstly, it didn't broadcast your credentials like you would when you talked to the P-Mac. Secondly, typing was probably half as fast, or less, and that was a small thing that helped to slow down any hacking attempts.

A while back, not long after he'd started at Valkyrie Machines, Ny had been exploring VM's security, and found a couple of these backdoors. Overtime he'd found a few more. Problem is, you couldn't scrub away everything you did, that would make you too obviously suspicious. So you had to be discreet and picky about what you chose to scrub. That meant that Ny had become less chatty over time. His mouth had always had a tendency to run off without him and it had gotten him in trouble during his varsity days. More than once.

So he'd taken to becoming quieter, and when he did speak, he hardly spoke about anything of any depth in most polite company. Polite company being a euphemism for the sniveling cowards that were all around him.

At home though, he'd taken to scrubbing pretty much everything because of how hard it was to govern himself accordingly, especially with him and El making love most nights and talking about all the things wrong with the world and how they'd change it if they could.

Anyway, in the beginning of his explorations of VM's backdoors, he'd found the master key server. This was where all logins were stored securely and encrypted. It hadn't really helped him to access this server. Encryption might have been compromised generally because of the GoE's overreach, but encryption used by the large corporations and government institutions was still untouched and therefore secure.

But that got him to thinking. He might not be able to access current user keys, but he found that he could create additional ones. So he did. The problem was, he was now down to his last user key which meant that he had to create others at the first opportunity he got.

User keys were the most difficult part to scrub and he wasn't certain he was able to scrub them properly all the time. At some point you had to log out with that user key and once you're out that last little logout crumb stood out like a sore thumb. What he'd been doing to circumvent that was to take that user key and hop it down to one of the lowest hierarchical servers before logging out. That meant that he could go back in under his own user key and scrub it away without anyone really noticing because it was on such a low security server that most people didn't give a Mars about and that wasn't audited with any real interest or regularity.

The pod started to slow and pull over.

"Juno, Jupiter and Mars," cursed Ny.

"Are you okay, darling?" asked El, before she realized what she had said.

Ny shot her a look and put his finger to his lips.

"Sorry," she mouthed.

Now he had another bit of scrubbing to do. At least he was still inside VM's servers but he was having a hard time finding the server he needed. He'd forgotten the path to it. He was fumbling around like a bumbling idiot and he was cursing himself under his breath.

He'd never had to access a server while under pressure. Usually he had oodles of time to do it while at work or at home where he felt like he had all the time in the world.

"Think, Mars dammit, Ny," he said under his breath.

The pod had now come to a stop. It was waiting for the mentor's pod. El put her hands around Ny's shoulders and started to give him a little encouraging massage.

One of the other reasons that Ny liked to use these private VM pods was the modicum of privacy they offered. Private pods didn't video record anything that happened within them. That was a special exception they had been granted from the GoE. Of course, it didn't offer a ton of privacy. Unlike the public pods, you had to have your P-Mac with you in order to access a VM pod.

You had to have your P-Mac with you for a public pod too. As you know, you needed to carry your P-Mac with you at all times. It was just that the public pods didn't check because A, they recorded everything with video and audio and B, your ticket was issued to you personally and that identified you when you entered the public pod. If you were using a standalone ticket.

The shoulder massage helped. He felt the tightness of his muscles start to relax and his typing became more accurate. He closed his eyes and thought for a moment as he retraced his steps the last time he'd accessed this server.

He tried again and then the correct path came to him almost instinctively through muscle memory. He was in the right server to scrub this vroom vroom's logs. He quickly swiped back to the location application. The mentor pod was just turning onto the street he was stopped on. He had maybe a minute to finish up. He felt the pressure mount once more.

The one bright spot with the situation he found himself in was the fact that mentors needed a hardline into the VM's pod portal in order to access the logs locally. Accessing logs from a pod required this mating rather than an air gapped handshake for security reasons. It gave him a little extra time. The mentors had to physically access this pod. They couldn't just sit in their cozy mentor pod and stream the information to them.

Ny found what he was looking for and started rewriting over it. But it was taking too long. He knew he had to use a different process. He had developed a variety of ways of dealing with logs of this sort. Back in the early days, he'd tried masking the audio with algorithms that distorted any voices so that they couldn't be deciphered. The problem was, these algorithms could be defeated over time.

But under current circumstances this was the best approach. And it would work so long as the mentors didn't decide to download the logs to their P-Macs to take away with them. In that case, who knew how long he had. He'd tested his algorithm on a piece of audio five minutes long, and he'd given up trying to break it after a week. But the mentors had more powerful machines to pit against his flimsy algorithm and he knew in time, how long that was he couldn't say, but in time, they'd break the algorithm and have access to the unaltered logs.

That was a risk, but it was something he had to live with. He didn't have the time to scrub all the logs before the mentors got to him. He tapped away and uploaded a bit of code to create a distortion in the voice logs. It didn't take long. El leaned into his ear.

"They've stepped out of their car," she said.

"Mars damn," he said under his breath.

He was almost done, he just needed to hop down a few servers to get out with his currently used user key.

Don't miss out!

Visit the website below and you can sign up to receive emails whenever Jason Blacker publishes a new book. There's no charge and no obligation.

https://books2read.com/r/B-A-RBB-XSLBB

BOOKS 2 READ

Connecting independent readers to independent writers.

Also by Jason Blacker

A Lady Marmalade Mystery
Beggar's Pardon
Sins of the Father
Gandhi's Sorrow
Phantoms of the Pharaoh
The Baron at Bishops Avenue
The Priest at Puddle's End
Lady Marmalade Cozy Murder Mysteries: Box Set (Books 1 - 3)
Four Red Diamonds (A Lady Marmalade Mystery 4 Pack)
Heartless
Loose Lips
Misery's Company
Poisoned Heart

An Anthony Carrick Mystery
Fourth Wall
Fifth Estate
Sixth Sense
Seventh Son
Brotherly Love
Anthony Carrick Hardboiled Murder Mysteries: Box Set (Books 1 - 3)
First Feature
Money Ain't Nothing
All In

Four Ways to Midnight
Second Fiddle
Third Base
Washed Up

Carbon Heart Silicon Soul
Jupiter: Book 1

Head Case Trilogy
Head Rush

TaXI Adventure
Ta.X.I. to Angola

Standalone
Can You Please Be Quiet
Dust on His Soul
Flowers For The Journey
Forever Famine
Livid Blue
My Son And I
Ruffled Feathers
Running Red River
When There Was One
Red Reign
The Enigma Evolution
Small Boy
Lady Marmalade Cozy Murder Mysteries: Box Set (Books 4 - 6)

Watch for more at JasonBlacker.com.

About the Author

Jason Blacker was born in Cape Town but spent most of his first 18 years in Johannesburg. When not grinding his fingers down to stubs at the keyboard he enjoys drinking tea, calisthenics and running. Currently he lives in Canada. Under his own name he writes hard boiled as well as cozy mysteries, action adventure, thrillers, literary fiction and anything else that tickles his muse. Jason Blacker also writes poetry and daily haikus at his haiku blog. You can find his haikus and other poetry at his website **www.haiqueue.com**. For FREE books and to stay up to date and learn about new releases be sure to visit **www.jasonblacker.com** where you can find more information about his writing and upcoming projects. If you enjoy space opera in the tradition of Star Trek then take a look at Jason Blacker's pen name "Sylynt Storme". It is under the name Sylynt Storme where you can find both sci-fi and vampire fiction written by Jason Blacker. "Star Sails" is the space opera series and "The Misgivings of the Vampire Lucius Lafayette" is his vampire series.

Read more at JasonBlacker.com.

www.ingramcontent.com/pod-product-compliance
Lightning Source LLC
Chambersburg PA
CBHW050900180626
46814CB00007B/2810

9 7 8 1 9 2 7 6 2 3 8 1 7